A MAX AHLGREN NOVEL

NEXUS

RYAN W. ASLESEN

ISBN 978-1-54398-155-1 - Ebook

ISBN 978-1-54398-154-4 – Paperback

Cover layout by Deranged Doctor Design www.derangeddoctordesign.com

Editing by: Tyler Mathis, Leigh Hogan, and Denise Fortowsky

www.ryanaslesen.com

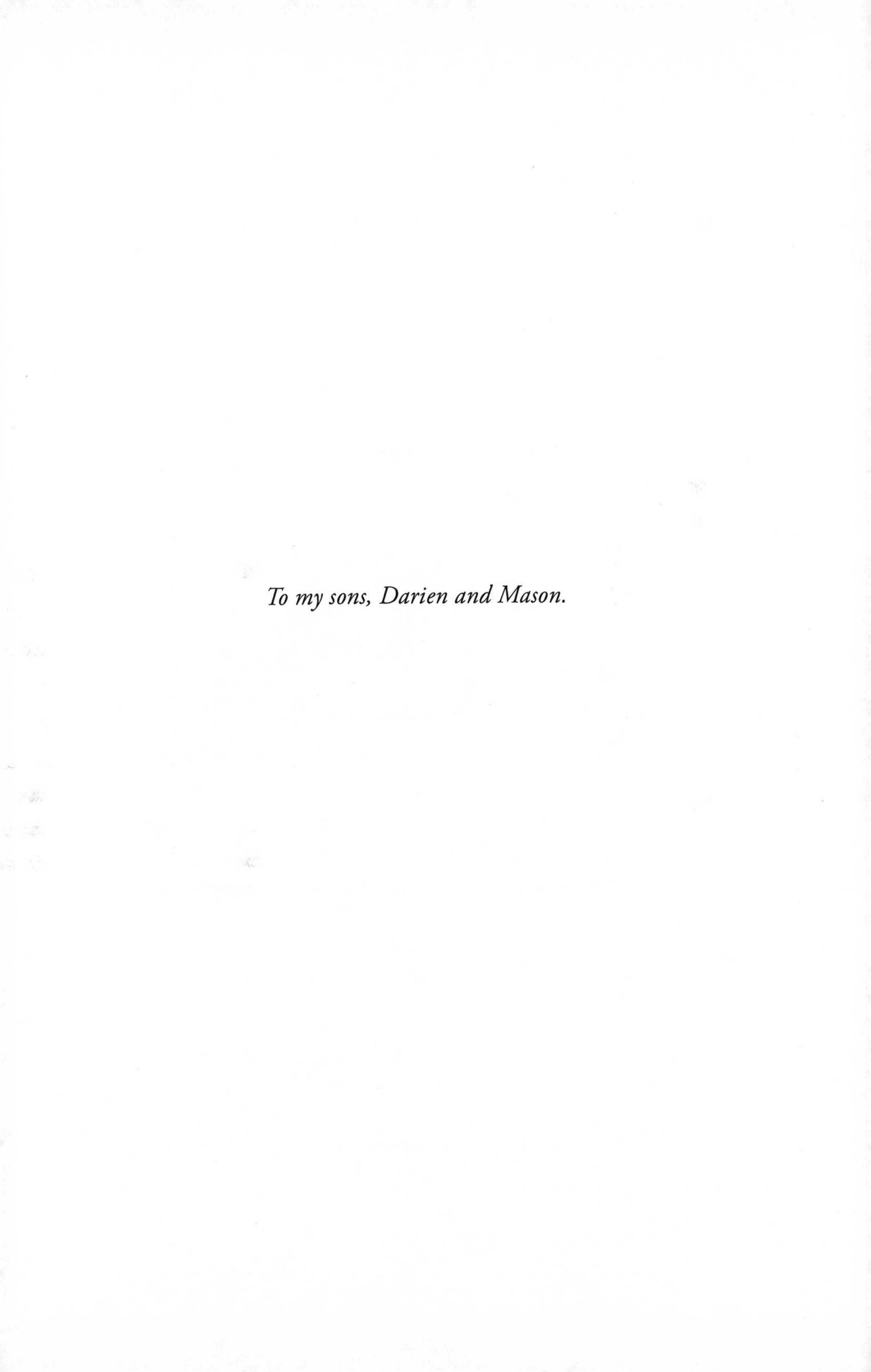

To my sons, Darien and Mason.

Acknowledgments

I would like to thank all the talented people who worked behind the scenes in connection with this book. A finished book is a culmination of hundreds of hours of work and a by-product of the collaboration of many talented people. This book would truly not be possible if it wasn't for their collective efforts.

Every writer needs an advocate, and I am particularly lucky to have the advice and assistance of my developmental editor, Tyler Mathis, a fellow Marine and brother-in-arms, for all his help and collaboration in producing this story. My stories wouldn't be what they are without your invaluable input and guidance.

I would also like to acknowledge the invaluable help given to me by Leigh Hogan in copy editing my manuscript. You are an encyclopedia of knowledge, and your time and effort is greatly appreciated. My work is all the better for it.

I would also like to thank Denise Fortowsky for her help with the final edit and proofread.

Any mistakes or shortcomings that remain in this book are mine and mine alone.

A book isn't complete without a cover, and I want to thank Kim and Darja with Deranged Doctor Design for the final cover design and marketing materials. You guys have been awesome, and I appreciate the great covers you continue to put together for me.

A heartfelt thanks also goes out to my readers. I appreciate you purchasing my books and taking the time to experience my stories. And a very special thanks to all of you who have extended kind words of positive support or left reviews and recommendations. It truly means a lot to me and my family. I continue to enjoy this amazing journey, and I'll keep writing these books as long as you keep buying them or pay me to stop.

Last, and most importantly, I want to thank my family for all their love and support.

He conquers who endures.

— *Persius*

1

Special Agent Margaret Leet, FBI, stared incredulously at the arrivals and departures monitor glowing above the entrance to the concourse at Los Angeles Union Station. *Shit, this is not good.*

"First wrench in the works," said her partner, Don Wagner. He had pasted on an expression of good-natured vexation for the benefit of their two charges. That hardly captured the sinking anxiety he felt in this situation.

The scientist, Daniel Farber, and his young son, Shai, had already endured trials beyond belief. They'd seen violence the average person could never comprehend. Showing downcast apprehension over the late train departure would only make them worry further. Leet and Wagner needed them to remain calm, optimistic and, above all, patient. They had crossed half the world on their own and would soon reach the safehouse outside of Washington DC with the help of the two FBI agents.

But they need to believe. They have to trust us. "So much for calling ahead," Leet said with a shrug and a strained smile.

Rather than calling, she'd checked the train's status on the internet before departing the hotel. Amtrak's eastbound *Sunset Limited* for New Orleans had been scheduled to depart LA on time at 10:00 pm, but things had changed during the fifteen-minute ride to Union Station. Departure time had been pushed back to 10:45 for some yet unknown reason. Their meticulously timed plan to escape LA—arrive a few minutes before departure, board immediately, and ensconce Farber and Shai in their sleeping car compartments away from watching eyes—had officially been shot to hell by what they could only hope was just shit luck. A shame, for it had been a good plan in Leet's estimation. LAX would certainly be staked out, along with the other major airports on the West Coast, and likely the Greyhound station as well. Not even driving would be safe according to Wagner. Operatives might be stationed at any number of rest areas and truck stops on the highways radiating from LA.

The train was Leet's idea. Her late father had been obsessed with railroads, and though she had no interest in trains herself, she believed rail travel would be the safest mode for beginning their journey. Few people traveled on long-distance trains anymore except for tourists and retirees, people with too much time on their hands. They would ride overnight, get off in El Paso the next afternoon to catch a flight to Atlanta, then switch planes for the final leg into DC. But for now, they would simply have to wait and remain hyper vigilant until they had Farber and son safely aboard the train.

"The waiting room is no good," Wagner muttered.

"Back outside?" Leet asked, though she didn't like the sound of that either.

"No. We'll hole up in here somewhere. It's a big building."

And old. This might work to their advantage. Union Station had been built in the waning days of grandiose American architecture, designed more with form in mind than function. Unlike the typically spare and utilitarian airport, it might offer any number of shady alcoves to hide in, or at least she hoped so.

"Let's get looking," Leet said.

"A moment, please, Margaret," said Farber. The agents had instructed Daniel and Shai to use their first names rather than their official titles, as though they were a tourist family on vacation. "Might we have a restroom break first?" he asked with careful and soft-spoken diction. He spoke English perfectly, without a trace of an Israeli accent, yet his halting manner of speech might have led some to believe he was a bit slow, though nothing could have been further from the truth. In the field of artificial intelligence, Daniel Farber was reputed to be the world's most gifted and brilliant scientist.

Leet looked to Wagner, who nodded. The restrooms were close by, down a short hallway to their right. "Sure thing," Leet said, smiling. "You guys head in; I'll wait outside with the luggage."

They walked the short distance to the restrooms. Leet, who could have used a bathroom break herself, remained in the hallway as Wagner led the way into the men's room. "Watch it, Don," she said quietly, keying her radio.

"You watch yourself, doll," Wagner responded into her earpiece, his voice dripping its usual confidence.

With his full head of dark hair, movie-star features and flawlessly fit body, Wagner might have been the poster boy for the ultimate G-man. He was so good looking that some of the older agents referred to him as Robert Wagner. Leet had googled the old-school actor, way before her time, and had to agree that there was a resemblance. With Don by her side, both on and off the job, she knew she couldn't lose. Leet's mother never failed to question her daughter regarding the relationship during their biweekly phone conversations, hopefully anticipating the day when Don might propose and give her a litter of grandkids that could find work in soap operas.

Leet reached beneath her brown leather jacket to loosen the Glock 23 in her shoulder holster, ensuring it would be ready for a quick draw. Digging into her purse, her hand brushed her second pistol, a Glock 27, as she reached for her vape pen. As in most of America, smoking was strictly prohibited in Union Station, probably punishable by drawing and quartering in the state of California, and this included vaping. But rush hour was long past, the station largely deserted. Security also appeared to have gone home, no guards lurking about to give her any shit. She hit the pen, felt the nicotine go to work almost instantaneously, and relaxed slightly.

As she stood there vaping, Leet watched a gray-bearded, middle-aged man wearing red Doc Martens approach, his tattered denim vest covered with patches and pins advertising punk rock bands that had broken up around the same time as the Soviet Union. She scrutinized him carefully from the corner of her eye, for all the good it did her. Wagner had warned her that this would be their most challenging assignment yet, for there were interests and operatives from several organizations and nations searching for Daniel Farber. His pursuers might be wearing any manner of dress or disguise, yet the old punk rocker only struck her as a legit loser who still thought himself in high school, not the sort to caution Wagner about.

What the hell is in that briefcase? It was the only piece of their luggage not sitting at her feet; Farber carried the thin metal case with him everywhere. It held the software for the project, of course, but what exactly did that entail? Even her top-secret clearance, capable of opening nearly any door in the halls of government, entitled her to no further information. And even Don, who kept no secrets from her, had declined to comment on the nature of the software.

That alone made her think that he was likewise in the dark. *Focus, damn it. Leave artificial intelligence to the expert.*

Footsteps clacking on the marble floor drew her attention to a tall older man carrying a leather briefcase, who was apparently headed for the men's room. His gray hair, fastidiously cut and styled, along with his tailored gray suit and ramrod posture immediately piqued her interest—he looked to be government at a glance. But was he? The suit looked a bit pricy even for a senior alphabet agent, and his cordovan wingtips probably cost more than she brought home in a month. He might be a lawyer or investment banker commuting home on one of the late suburban trains. Leet paid careful attention to his form-fitting suit jacket, looking for the telltale bulge of a pistol in a shoulder holster. *Looks clean. Pity I can't x-ray that briefcase.* She shook her head slightly at the futility of trying to catch shit before it hit the metaphorical fan.

The train departure time couldn't come soon enough. She checked her watch: 9:58. The PA system crackled as the final boarding call for the *Texas Chief*, bound for Chicago, was announced. *We chose the wrong—*

Sounds of a scuffle emanated from the men's room. Something went *thump*, and Wagner's lone, shouted word cut through the steel bathroom door: "Shit!"

The vape pen dropped from Leet's fingers. She drew her piece and charged into the men's room, small for a railroad station, decorated in a once-colorful display of tiles arranged in a Southwestern motif. She caught a glimpse of the gray-suited man standing at the far end of the room, but before she could react, the aged punk threw her into the wall with a swipe of his arm and bolted from the restroom.

A single, cracking shot from an unsilenced pistol—Wagner's—echoed off dingy ceramic tiles, accompanied by the sound of a mirror shattering. He lay on his back, bleeding from the neck as he pointed his pistol upward for another shot at the phony lawyer, who towered over him with a silenced pistol in hand. Farber sprawled next to him on the floor, dazed and bleeding from a laceration on his face, his metal briefcase lying at the older man's feet. Shai was nowhere to be seen.

It never crossed Leet's mind to make an arrest—this mission was strictly shoot to kill. The target stood in profile, just beginning to turn and face her. She raised the Glock and aimed for his head, jerking the trigger in a hasty rush of adrenaline. Her round struck him high in the shoulder of his gun arm; a misty puff of blood spurted forth to airbrush a sink. He grunted, dropped his gun, which Wagner had the presence of mind to knock away with a flailing leg as he sighted in for another shot.

Showing surprising speed and agility for a man his age, one polished Oxford kicked Wagner in the groin as the man in the gray suit darted toward a stall to take cover. Combined with the pain from his gunshot wound, the agony of the blow knocked Wagner unconscious.

Leet fired again, a poorly timed shot that struck the wall where the man had been. The ricocheting round pinged about the bathroom like a supersonic pinball.

The man bent over and grabbed Farber's metal briefcase, stepped from the stall, and flung it straight at her head. The move caught her completely by surprise and forced her to duck. She saw nothing but expensive gray fabric when she looked up again, gun raised, as he slammed an elbow into her chin, a hit that rattled her teeth, brought stars to her eyes, and put her on the floor.

Leet shook her head, her grogginess dissipating. She rolled until she saw Farber's briefcase on the floor not three feet away. The man's exquisitely manicured right hand seized the carry handle. Leet raised her pistol clumsily. Perhaps his blow had left her more dazed than she realized, for he anticipated that move. When he stomped down hard on her right wrist with the heel of his Italian leather shoe, she cried out in pained surprise. Before she knew it, her fingers clutched only emptiness. He knocked her Glock into a urinal, kicked Leet in the ribs, then turned to depart with his stolen goods.

Fail! To Margaret Leet the word was unconscionable, always had been, even before the FBI Academy, and from somewhere deep within rose the fortitude to make one last attempt to foil this mysterious and deadly operative. Atop her purse, she couldn't grab her other gun, so in desperation she flung out both arms and locked her fingers tightly around the briefcase.

With both hands, the man yanked furiously at the carry handle but only succeeded in lifting Leet's dead weight. "Get the fuck off!" he spat, lashing out with a kick that narrowly missed her head.

"How bad do you want it, dick?" She grinned up at him spitefully.

He responded with a primal growl of frustration through gritted teeth; then he bent over and lifted his trouser leg to expose another pistol in an ankle holster. Leet doubled her efforts and wrenched the briefcase from his left hand.

But it would all be for naught, she realized when she stared into the seemingly bottomless bore of his backup pistol. The man's maniacal eyes, a slightly darker shade of gray than his suit, gleamed over the sights.

Then they both heard the faint and distant shouts of people panicking from the gunfire. He quickly turned away from Leet, shoved the pistol in his belt holster, and exited the bathroom. A shoulder wound like his would certainly draw unwanted attention. He would be out a side door and gone before security reached the area, vanished like a gray ghost at first light, though she didn't believe she'd seen the last of him.

Leet went to Wagner, ignoring Farber as he groaned on the floor next to him. At a glance she could tell that he'd already lost several pints of blood through the wound on his neck, a grazing shot that must have nicked an artery. "Fuck, fuck!" she babbled in panic. Untangling her purse from behind her back, she produced a handkerchief and pressed down hard on the wound. The cloth became saturated and useless within a few seconds. Blood sluiced through her fingers.

Wagner turned an odd blue-gray, the color of dirty ice. He convulsed for a moment, then opened his eyes.

"Get a medic in here!" Leet shouted, hoping to be heard over the hubbub that grew closer as the seconds passed.

"Don't bother," Wagner said in the faintest whisper.

"Jesus, Don, just hold on! Couple of minutes—"

"No." He shivered. "Anyone... like... told you." His eyes closed, the final curtain. "Trust... no one." With his last breath he uttered his final, unnecessary words.

It was too much—she could look upon her dead partner and lover no longer. Sobbing, she turned away from the man who had been Special Agent Don Wagner.

Shai stood before her, clutching the stuffed rabbit that rarely left his hands. Sadness lined his swarthy face beneath unruly locks of black hair, yet he shed no tears. Leet figured he must have hidden in a stall during the battle. Despite her grief, she couldn't help but marvel at the boy's composure. To her recollection, never once had he cried out in fear during the ordeal.

2

When someone envisions hell it usually involves fire, lava, tormented souls dancing about in eternal damnation as demons jabbed them in the ass with pitchforks. *Those people never spent a morning trekking through the Florida jungle.* Max Ahlgren paused to remove and stow his GPNVG-18 panoramic night vision goggles, one of the few pieces of tactical gear he'd brought along. The mosquitoes, voracious enough while he'd been moving, now descended on any bare skin they could find to feast in earnest, insect repellent be damned. Sweat popped and trickled from every pore in response to the stagnant, stifling humidity.

Could have been much worse, he supposed. *I could be doing this with a full combat load like we had to at Camp Gonsalves.*

He felt rather naked, actually, accustomed as he was to beginning his missions laden with over a hundred pounds of weapons, ammo, explosives, rations, and miscellaneous gear. But that much gear would have slowed him. His purpose this morning was to subdue and capture, rather than the usual seek and destroy, and required weapons he didn't normally carry: pepper spray, a million-volt stun baton, and a rag saturated with chloroform that he kept in a zip-lock bag in his cargo pocket. Non-lethal toys. His target would be armed, pissed off, and extremely dangerous, so he'd brought his Glock 21, Ka-Bar combat knife, and four extra magazines of ammo in case he needed to save his skin. Instead of his usual combat-load plate carrier, he'd opted for a low-visibility model worn beneath the camo hunting suit he'd purchased upon arriving in Florida. "Matches the local woods better than any other pattern," the salesman at the big-box outdoor store had assured him. "The turkey hunters round these parts swear by it."

"Good," Max had responded. "Because that's just what I'm after." *The biggest turkey of them all.*

Like that wary and elusive wild bird, Max's quarry, Swift Carter, possessed incredibly heightened senses. Surprising him on his own property would be a challenge; taking him alive even more so. As much as Max desired to kill the man, Swift was no good to him dead. First, they needed to have a little talk regarding a certain incident.

Max drank what remained of the electrolyte water in his hydration pack as first light intensified in the overcast sky, dimly illuminating woods of palmetto and pine with the thick trunks of cypress intervening in the many boggy depressions. Quicksand had been his primary concern when traversing this area during his recon. Even a man of his size and strength—6'4" and well over two hundred and thirty pounds—would have a hard time freeing himself from a mire.

He resumed his trek, moving as quietly as possible. The dwarf palmettos covering the forest floor precluded total stealth, however. Fortunately, millions of insects and dozens of birds had his back, singing their morning songs loudly enough to eclipse the noise of his movements.

Soon, he approached the tree line that marked the boundary of

Swift's property. There was no perimeter fence. Swift lived off the grid and generated his own power, but he hadn't the juice to electrify a lengthy fence. And a normal chain-link fence, even topped with razor wire, would only inconvenience a true professional—the only sort who would come after Swift—so why bother erecting one? To ward off unwanted guests, Swift posted his property with slightly altered no trespassing signs. On each one, the generic warning line of *violators will be prosecuted to the fullest extent of the law* had been crossed out with black marker and replaced with scrawled black letters reading: **Violators will deal with me!** Max could only imagine what that might entail. Swift was capable of dishing out any number of grisly punishments.

Max drew his pistol, dropped to the prone position, and low-crawled the last few feet to the edge of the woods. The view was familiar by now: a field of knee-high grass and weeds giving way to a pond surrounded by a low chain-link fence meant to keep the occupants, several alligators of varying sizes, from running amok on the property. A narrow canal perhaps ten feet across flowed into one end of the pond and out the other through thick metal grating. Through unkempt ornamental palms, Max glimpsed the glint of water in two other ponds. He knew from satellite imagery that there were six ponds altogether connected by the canal, which flowed to the swamp that backed up to the property. Not even Swift Carter could prevent Google Earth from invading his private domain. A well-trodden footpath ran alongside the near pond's fence, and all the ponds featured a platform built over the water at one end for feeding and observation.

The house and a couple of outbuildings were located on the other side of the property, which Max had reconned as well. Swift's dogs had gone apeshit when they'd picked up his unfamiliar scent, but no one had been home at the time.

He knew the general layout of the place well enough. And he knew the time was right.

Upon arriving in Florida, Max had hidden a motion-activated wireless video camera in the brush across the road from the gate to Swift's mile-long driveway. Swift's wife, Imogene, left the premises six mornings a week at around 0415 to open their bait and tackle shop. The shop was closed on Mondays, but today was Tuesday, so she would be at work. Max had seen no sign of Swift until two days previous, when he arrived home from wherever he'd gone, probably on a merc job, though he claimed to be retired.

While waiting for Swift as the days dragged by, Max considered infiltrating the farm while Imogene was working but had opted not to. Paranoid as he was, Swift probably had video surveillance cameras posted all over his property or perhaps employed other old-school methods to detect trespassers. Max couldn't take the chance. If Swift had even the faintest idea that Max was coming, he would never be able to take the man on his home turf.

This is it. He'd waited so long for this moment to finally deal justice to one of the men who had helped murder his wife and young son. *And he's only the first.*

Flat as a tabletop, the field was roughly fifty yards across. Max started low crawling, taking his time, bound for a patch of stunted palms near the feeding platform. Upon reaching the palms, he came to his knees in the sand for a look around. Not surprisingly, he spotted a video camera mounted high on a palm tree adjacent to the water inside the fence, pointed toward the sandy path. *How many haven't I seen?* Hopefully, Swift wasn't in the house hunched over the monitors right now.

As he pondered his next move, Max heard a faint yet guttural voice from nearby that put his worries to rest. A moment later, the smell of putrefaction assaulted his nostrils. Had to be feeding time for the gators. Swift was partial to filet mignon, but the gators had less distinguished palates.

Max stood, darting across a patch of overgrown grass to another copse of dwarf palms to get a good look at the next pond. There, on the end of the ramshackle feeding platform, stood the massive silhouette of Swift, his back turned to Max, a once-white plastic bucket stained the color of blood at his feet. He stood slightly shorter than Max, and the breadth of his shoulders made him seem almost as wide as he was tall. A filthy white t-shirt, tucked into a pair of tattered camo cargo shorts, strained to contain his bulk—brawny muscles secreted beneath a thick layer of fat. He wore no shoes but would never have left the house without strapping on a weapon or two. The leather gun belt around his waist held a combat knife and a blued high-caliber revolver, an old Smith & Wesson with classic walnut grips and at least an eight inch barrel.

Swift loved only three things in life: reptiles, vintage guns, and for some reason, his fat and rather homely wife. But reptiles had come long before the others. Henry Carter grew up at a Florida tourist trap, a squalid roadside reptile zoo not far from his present farm. Huge from day one, at the age of fourteen he began wrestling alligators under the name Gator Hank, entertaining crowds of tourists until his father, a noted herpetologist, drank the zoo into bankruptcy. After that he enlisted in the army, matriculated to the Green Berets, and eventually became a CIA field operative, where he earned his facetious moniker. Due to his monumental size, he tended to move slower in the field than his comrades, though in a fight—particularly hand-to-hand—he could still strike faster than any alligator.

Max first met Swift during his time with the CIA. They'd never gotten along, each man fancying himself the better leader. Twice they butted heads while working counterterrorism missions and would have come to blows once, had they not been separated by other operatives. Their rivalry resumed when Max left the CIA for a career as a private security contractor, the same field Swift had entered upon leaving the Agency several years prior. He was no less cold-blooded than the beasts he loved so dearly. When Swift had the chance to be his own boss, he gave his callous nature free rein.

Less than a year before, Max, Swift, and three other men infiltrated and destroyed a research facility run by the infamous rogue geneticist Gideon Wilde, located on an island off the coast of French Guiana. Wilde escaped, alas, but as reward for taking down the operation, Max learned the identity of one of the men who had murdered his family.

And here we are.

From the bucket, Swift removed a piece of carrion, slimy with dripping blood, some sort of disgusting organ from a prey animal.

"Come on over here, Betsy, old girl," he called across the pond.

An alligator roughly fifteen feet long, this pond's only occupant, gained its stubby legs on the far bank. It trotted to the water, entered with nary a splash, and cruised across the pond like a patrolling submarine, only its yellow, unfeeling eyes visible.

"That's it, girl, come on." Swift dangled the gator's reeking breakfast over the platform's edge. "Open up. Talk to me, Betsy. You know you gotta speak."

A groan like a giant's burp emanated from below the platform.

"Good girl!" Swift dropped the stinking offal, after which Max heard a sizeable splash. Chuckling with amused satisfaction, Swift reached into the bucket for more food. This time Betsy sounded off without hesitation, eliciting laughter from Swift.

Damn shame. If you'd worked your way through college and become a herpetologist, we wouldn't have to go through all this.

Max allowed Swift to feed Betsy, which took a couple of minutes. Still hungry, Betsy groaned to no avail, then started splashing around.

“That’s all of it, girl. You know how it works.”

Max used her noise to cover his movement as he stepped from the palmettos and onto the path, the red dot in his reflex sight aimed just to the left of Swift’s spine, poised for a heart shot if need be. “Hands up, Carter!”

Swift went rigid. “Ahlgren. Finally found your stealth, I see.” As he spoke, his right hand crept toward the Smith’s butt.

“Don’t even think it. You’re not fast enough.” Max advanced a few steps.

“Can’t argue that.” His hands went into the air.

“Take that gun belt off, nice and slow.”

“What the hell’s this about?”

“The gun belt, asshole. Make it happen.”

“Okay.”

Max stepped onto the platform as Swift unbuckled the leather belt. “Hold it over your head.” Swift complied. “Now toss it in the pond.”

Swift balked at the order and flinched. “Aw come on, Max, not my Model 29.”

“’Fraid so, Dirty Harry.”

“Well, shit.” With no choice but to part with his .44, Swift flung the belt into the water. Betsy lunged toward the splash.

“Now turn around slowly.” Swift’s front half was no more appealing than his rear. Beneath an iron-gray flattop, sweat beaded on his forehead, whether from the humidity or the moment of truth, Max couldn’t say. Almost as ugly as his beloved wife, Swift’s blunt, jowly face looked like something a kindergartner might have sculpted from lumps of clay.

“Can I put my hands down now?” he asked.

“If you can keep ’em out of your pockets.”

“I might just.”

Max ignored his ambiguous response. "You know why I'm here."

Swift managed to look remorseful, even sad. Max couldn't have given a shit less about his emotions. "Yeah. I knew this day would come. Who told you? Marklin?"

Max didn't respond.

"Yeah, that's about what I thought, fuckin' shady old jarhead. You should put him to the question."

"It's crossed my mind." Thomas Marklin, a retired Marine Corps lieutenant general and former liaison to the CIA, had inducted Max into the Agency thirteen years before. For that reason alone, Max didn't wholly trust the man. These days Marklin worked for some sort of think tank/security firm in DC that catered to high-level government officials. He also served as Max's informant, a DC insider who had a little dirt on just about everybody.

Swift chuckled, spat a stream of tobacco juice over the platform's rotting, rickety railing. "You think I'm the only one he knows about?"

"Maybe. Maybe not. And right now, I don't give a shit. I know for certain that you were on Jarvis' team."

This time Swift guffawed, his stout gut shaking in time to his mirth. "Jarvis, eh? That ain't his real name, you know."

"Then what is it?"

Swift's face went flat, then grimly hostile. "Go ask Marklin."

"Not necessary. You'll tell me soon enough. I'll also have the names of the other two pieces of shit on that squad."

"Cleghorn's already dead, not that that was his real name."

"Thought so." Max had harbored suspicions regarding Cleghorn, a CIA operative he'd met on the Guyana mission, who seemed to recognize Max even though they had never met before. When Max last saw him, Cleghorn was lying in a wrecked French jeep, his body riddled with dozens of 9mm holes. Swift had gunned him down for no apparent reason. Not apparent at the time anyway.

"Maybe you should thank me. Consider it repentance for my sins."

"If you want to repent, give me two other names. You're gonna give 'em up anyway; whether we do this the easy or hard way is up to you."

Swift shrugged his ox-like shoulders. "I like things as easy as the next guy."

"Then tell me their names right now. If I believe you, I'll put a slug in your forehead, quick and merciful. I'll even feed you to Betsy if you'd like."

Swift took a step forward, then another. "And let me guess: the hard way is you chaining me to a chair and toasting my balls with a blowtorch."

"If you're lucky. I've stepped up my torture game as of late. Practice makes perfect."

"Sorry to disappoint you, Max, but neither option works for me. I'm not goin' anywhere with you unless I'm in a rubber bag... if you think you can put me in one."

"I can, and that's far enough, Carter."

Swift had continued his slow and—in his mind, perhaps—surreptitious advance. They now stood about ten feet from one another. His grin burned red with tobacco juice. "My ranch, my rules. Shoot me if you like, but the secrets die with me."

"Bring it." Max holstered his gun and took up the stun baton.

Swift closed the last few feet and lunged for him with outstretched hands like two sides of beef. He could ruthlessly tear a man apart with his bare hands—Max had seen him do it. Getting to the fight was his weakness. Max feinted right, darted left, and drove the stun baton into Swift's ribs before he could grab it in one of his meaty hands. Electricity discharged with a crackling pop. Grunting, Swift twitched and veered to the right, hitting the railing. The rotten wood yielded beneath his weight, the crack loud as a pistol shot, yet somehow the railing held.

The high-voltage charge would have dropped most men but not the likes of Swift Carter. Down but not out as Max descended on him with the baton, he caught Max's right wrist in both hands. The end of the baton crackled as Max involuntarily pressed the trigger button in response to Swift's vice-like grip. Max tried to drive a left into his face, but Swift heaved a mighty shove and pushed him away before he could connect, driving him back several feet.

To his alarm, Max realized he was now the one cornered on the platform.

Swift advanced, slow and wary this time. With his left hand, Max pulled the pepper spray cannister from his belt, raised it, and shot a stream at Swift's face that flew over his head as he ducked and charged. Max triggered another stream that caught Swift right in the eyes an instant before he plowed into him. The platform shook when they went down in a tangle, Swift growling in agonized rage over his burning eyes. But he kept his discipline, didn't try to rub the spray away, which would only drive it further into his eyes and pores. He still had the upper hand as he lay atop Max, who drove the baton into his ribs once more, delivering a one-second discharge that rolled Swift off him.

Now back in command, Max got to his knees and aimed another baton thrust at Swift's gut as he lay there blinded and reeling. But blindness and pain were only minor obstacles to a man of Swift's fortitude and training. Though he had only a vague idea of where Max might be, he launched a vicious kick that caught Max on the chin and sent him reeling backward, darkness enveloping his consciousness in the moment before he crashed into the platform railing. The warped gray wood gave a little beneath his weight and momentum, cracked once, but did not shatter. Max shook his head, tried to clear the bursting fireworks from behind his eyelids.

A wrecking ball slammed into Max's solar plexus, driving the air from his lungs, followed by a wicked uppercut that snapped his head back. His mind swam with vertigo, as though he were drifting in outer space.

From somewhere he heard, "Like them stun batons, eh?"

Max twisted to evade the baton to no avail. The sting in his ribs made him pop and twitch, his incapacitation complete. He pressed the trigger button on the pepper spray, only to find he'd dropped the canister. Swift jabbed him in the neck with the stun baton, laughed, then drove one of his beefy knees into Max's balls.

Max felt as though every neuron in his body had overloaded and short-circuited. His vertigo took on new dimensions, physical dimensions, as he felt Swift first pull him forward, only to shove him backward an instant later. The railing shattered with a final mighty crack.

Falling! It was like a dream. He needed to awaken before he hit the ground.

Water enveloped Max in a cooling embrace, shocking him from his dazed torpor. He gasped, inhaled slimy, shit-ridden pond water, felt himself drowning as he flipped over. His boot soles embedded in the sandy bottom. He pushed with his legs and exploded to the surface, found himself standing in about five feet of water.

Swift leaned through the sundered railing, the baton poised above his head, a homicidal smile on his face. "Here, maybe this'll help, ya fuckin' dipshit!"

Still coughing up water, Max raised his forearm and steered the thrown baton aside, yet another bruise for the day's failed efforts.

Swift finger whistled. "Git him, Betsy!"

Oh shit... Max turned from the platform, saw the top of Betsy's head as she swam lazily in his direction. He pulled his Glock, put the red dot between her golden, gleaming eyes, and squeezed the trigger.

The pistol only clicked when the firing pin came down.

"Fuck!"

"Yeah, fuck is right, dumbass." Swift guffawed, then whistled again. "Eat him up, girl!"

Water rippled behind Betsy as she wriggled her thick tail just beneath the surface, gaining speed to seize her meal.

Max ejected the defective round, aimed once more, fired.

Click!

Betsy closed to within a few feet, then doubled her speed.

Max thought of his Ka-Bar. *Not enough!* Despite his prowess at knife fighting, facing Betsy with the combat knife would be a fool's errand. He might as well stick her with a toothpick. He wracked the slide once more, ejected the wet round, prayed, and fired into Betsy's face as her maw sprang open to devour his head, the carrion stench of her breath nauseating him. He heard nothing but the groan from deep in her gullet, saw nothing but pink tongue and piercing spikes of browning yellow teeth.

Never had the single pop of a gunshot brought such relief. The bullet took her high in the back of her mouth, penetrating the soft flesh to find her tiny reptilian brain, which it blasted into mush before lodging in her thick skull. The round's impact barely budged her great weight. Her jaws closed gently, for the last time, mere inches from Max's face.

Betsy floated before him like a torpedoed dreadnaught, slowly rolling belly up, her tail end starting to sink.

Max stood there; feet planted in sandy muck as he caught his breath. "Don't sweat it, Betsy. All the girls say I taste like shit."

Swift. Max turned to the platform, found it empty, caught a glimpse of Swift fleeing down the path leading to his house. "You better run, you piece of shit!" Max made for the bank to pick up the chase, his quest to take Carter alive forgotten. The luxury of savoring this revenge had come and gone.

3

After chasing Swift halfway around the chain of ponds, Max reached a fork in the path. The left fork ended at Swift's house but down the right fork, Swift ran for the swamp with a shuffling, elephantine gait, bound for the rickety dock where he kept his airboat tied up. Max, in far better shape, gained on him. Less than a hundred yards separated them now. He figured he could get in range and take out Swift before he escaped.

A hot wind laden with lead and smelling of cordite blew past his back. Max grunted when something like a hornet stung him in the shoulder. He turned, saw Imogene standing on the concrete patio before the house, wearing a soiled housedress and holding a double-barreled shotgun. *Dammit!* He ran to take cover behind the massive trunk of a live oak, felt again the wind and whistle of buckshot, though none of the pellets struck him.

He reached the oak, then leaned out from cover with his pistol leveled toward the porch. Somehow he retracted his head a heartbeat before the next shotgun blast tore into the trunk, kicking up a storm of splinters. "Shit!" It felt as though fire ants feasted on his face. *How the fuck did she reload so fast?* Perhaps he'd been mistaken; maybe she had a semi-auto shotgun instead of a double barrel. Conscious of each wasted second, Max stuck out his gun arm and retracted it an instant before Imogene's next shot roared past. He then stepped from behind the tree, got his reflex sight on her as she broke open and reloaded with great speed, her shotgun shells held ready between splayed fingers. Just as she snapped the breech closed with a flick of her ample wrist, Max fired a single shot that took her high in the chest, knocking her back into the house's open front doorway.

He had no idea why she was home, not that it mattered now. He looked to the dock. Oily smoke puffed from the airboat's exhaust as Swift cranked the ignition. Max took off at a sprint, running the most crucial hundred-yard dash of his life.

He was fifty yards away when the engine turned over in a cloud of white smoke, quickly blown away by the fan. "Motherfucker!" He fired wildly at the boat as Swift cranked up the fan and pulled away from the dock. A bullet sparked as it pinged off the fan housing; another ricocheted off the aluminum hull. Max halted, sighted in carefully on the airboat's engine as Swift gunned it. The spray kicked up by the fan obscured his view at the last instant, ruining the shot.

Bellowing rage, Max emptied the magazine in the general direction of the diminishing boat, striking nothing important, as Swift took off for parts unknown.

Thoroughly disgusted with his failed efforts, Max paused on the path to collect himself and ponder his next move. He put a fresh magazine into the Glock and chambered a round. But for the groaning of a distant alligator and the sound of thunder from a far-off lightning strike, silence reigned on the farm.

Max figured he would find interesting things in the spacious outbuilding of corrugated metal in the back yard. *But fuck it; start with the house, maybe there's something there.* What that something might be, he had no idea.

First, he had to take care of Imogene, if she required it.

Max trudged to the house, typical of residential structures in Florida: a single story of concrete block with a flat roof, garishly painted a light mint-green trimmed with red. Unlike most homes, bars adorned all of the windows. Confined in a pen out back, Swift's three bloodhounds howled and bayed.

He could tell from twenty feet away that Imogene wouldn't be getting up again. His shot had taken her dead center in the chest, just above her fat, pendulous tits. Her blue eyes stared up at the porch overhang; pooled blood clotted in her cascade of greasy brown hair.

Her shotgun lay on the concrete beside her. Max's eyes bugged when he saw the intricate engraving on the breech, the craftsmanship of the wooden stock and foregrip. *Holy shit, a Prussian Daly.* Only at Swift's house would someone try to end him with a $5,000 shotgun.

"You should have gone to work today." He dragged her body into the living room through the open front door.

The motif of Swift's living room could best be described as white trash wins the lottery. His black leather furniture and mahogany tables were of high quality and had probably cost him a few bills. A TV of at least 75" dominated most of one wall. A spacious wire cage housing a long green iguana took up another. A cold pellet stove sat in one corner, waiting patiently to combat one of Florida's rare winter cold snaps.

Despite the grandeur of the décor, the place was a fucking mess, a chamber of clutter and filth. Junk food wrappers, empty cans of Red Dog beer, and overflowing ashtrays littered dirty shag carpeting from the 1970s. The cracked and peeling paint, once white, was tinged a dingy tan from decades of cigarette smoke.

Swift, a non-smoker, had placed an antique spittoon next to his favorite chair, the oxidized brass green from want of polish. Max smiled. Déjà vu had struck. *Just the way I always pictured it.*

Though he wanted to thoroughly toss the entire house, Max knew he didn't have all day. Swift would return, probably at the head of an angry redneck posse with itchy trigger fingers. He might even decide to fetch the law. Max figured Imogene would cost him at least forty years in prison, if not a lethal injection. The living room wasn't likely to yield any useful information, so he moved on in search of a more likely space such as a home office.

He navigated through the unsanitary kitchen and down a hallway, opting to skip Swift's bedroom, which smelled of more ass than a locker room after a college football game. He didn't even want to ponder what might have transpired in that chamber of horrors.

He found the cramped office, little more than a walk-in closet, located in a back corner of the house. Two display racks of vintage long guns hung on the walls, beautiful examples of the finest rifles and shotguns ever made—Beretta, Weatherby, another Daly. Max appreciated the quality workmanship, but past that they did not interest him. He collected military firearms exclusively.

Swift's desk consisted of a six-foot plastic table with folding legs, its surface obscured beneath disheveled piles of paperwork and a laptop computer. Max moved the mouse, woke the computer from sleep, finding access restricted by a pin number. *Shit, I'll have to take it with me to get cracked.* A thought occurred to him. *Worth a shot.* He moved to the filing cabinet, also locked, and spent a couple of minutes prying open the drawers with his Ka-Bar. Quickly scanning the tabs on the files, he found the Carters' tax returns, both business and personal.

"Here we go." He sat at the table, felt his knee bump something beneath it. Swift had duct-taped a holster to the underside of the table. Max pulled out the revolver, an old .44 snub-nose bulldog, then returned it to the holster. *He probably has guns hidden all over the house.* Typical enough, Max did the same thing. In their line of work, Judgement Day might come any time.

Consulting last year's tax returns, he typed Imogene's birthday, 31576, into the box, and laughed when the computer unlocked.

"Fucking idiot." But he wasn't about to complain of Imogene's laziness in choosing her obvious pin number.

Within a minute he realized the computer would be a dead end. It contained little else but the books and files for their two legitimate businesses: the tackle shop and Swift's venom business. Max scanned the receipts. *I'm in the wrong line of work.* Swift made thousands of dollars per vial peddling snake venom to pharmaceutical companies that made antivenom and other medicines. Their legit businesses earned more than enough to obscure the money trail from Swift's illegitimate work as a mercenary. Max found no entries in the books regarding those payments, though he knew Swift had been paid a full half-mil in cash for the Guyana mission.

Max closed the computer, stood, and opened the closet. "Thought so." A rusting safe about a hundred years old sat on the floor beneath hanging clothing, which included a couple of Swift's old army uniforms. Locked, of course, and Swift wasn't foolish enough to use his birthday as a combination.

I'll get it open.

Max exited the house through the kitchen, stopping briefly to nab a ring of keys hanging on a hook next to the back door. His presence angered Swift's bloodhounds as he jogged to the metal outbuilding. He opened the thick steel door with one of the keys and stepped into an orderly workshop. Swift's truck, a brand-new black Dodge Ram with dualies on the back and a full gun rack in the rear window, sat center stage.

The vehicle didn't interest Max, who stared in awe at the machine gun on the workbench—an old German MG34 that Swift had been tinkering with. "Come to papa." The MG was fully assembled. *Hope all the parts are in it.* He slung it over his shoulder to add to his personal collection of legendary military weapons, then moved on to the two closed doors in the back wall.

The lady or the tiger? He chose the left door, which accessed a lab space of concrete and steel as opposed to the usual sterile white tile. A spartan space, clean and well organized, it housed a steel table, refrigerator, and snake handling implements on the left wall. The right had two rolling carts, each loaded with a dozen plastic tubs a foot high and about three feet long. Twelve reptile terrariums lined the far wall, with snakes visible in several. An electric space heater kept the place uncomfortably warm.

Each of the tubs—translucent, yet cloudy enough to obscure their occupants—was labeled with a Latin taxonomical binomial, scribed in a meticulous cursive hand that Max found difficult to attribute to a ham-fisted brute like Swift. He read a few of the names: *Micrurus fulvius, Crotalus adamanteus, Agkistrodon piscivorus*, none of whom he wished to meet. A quick check of the fridge revealed snake venom in various hues of yellow contained in beakers and vials, all likewise labeled, and not at all what he sought.

The other door, which he unlocked with a barrel key, accessed a concrete bunker containing Carter's work weapons, combat gear, and thousands of rounds of ammunition. Unlike Max, Swift employed classic, time-tested weapons as opposed to the latest firepower. Every warrior had his preferences. Max found explosives in government-issue wooden crates: square sticks of TNT, grenades of several varieties, white blocks of C-4 plastic explosive. *Jackpot.*

He returned to the house with an ALICE pack, a block of C-4, blasting caps, and a digital timer, as well as a five-gallon jerry can of gasoline from the workshop. The safe would not be budged, so he wired it where it stood, set the timer for thirty seconds, and waited in the kitchen. The explosion shook the slab foundation. Not surprisingly, the blast flipped the table and set the piles of paperwork in the office afire. The paper that mattered, however, remained intact within the safe, $775,000 in cash, which Max hurriedly stuffed into the backpack along with a flintlock pistol several hundred years old, likely the gem of Swift's extensive collection. He would get it appraised and then sell it when he returned home to Las Vegas.

The rest was simply arson. Max soaked the dirty carpets with gasoline. The office, now nicely afire, would provide the spark. He would leave no fingerprints behind. Blowing Swift's workshop proved ridiculously easy, requiring nothing more than another block of C-4 wired up next to the explosives in the munitions room. Max set the timer for one minute and hauled ass.

Though well clear of the shop when the building exploded, the concussion nevertheless knocked Max to the grass as he fled. He suffered no damage other than ringing ears, however, as bits of debris rained down nearby. The house went up in a ball of fire as he made his way off the property, around the ponds and back the way he'd come, moving double time. A column of black smoke had already climbed high into the sky, visible for miles over the flat Florida landscape. *I hope you see it, Swift, wherever you ran off to.*

The law would be along shortly to investigate.

Max pondered his failed mission as he ran through the slicing fronds of the palmetto jungle.

Though Swift had eluded him, they would certainly meet again. *He'll be gunning for me now.* But Max had no intention of letting him take the offensive. *I'll be back in your face before you know it.* Locating him again wouldn't be so easy, however. Max would require assistance and not through the usual channels. Marklin had given him Swift's name, but Max doubted he would help search for him. Max would check his contacts when he got to safety, figure out who still owed him, a list of men that grew shorter all the time as he called in more favors, mostly to no avail.

He turned to check his six and catch one last glimpse of Swift's burning property in the distance through the grove of trees. *That was a real goat fuck op, Max. Real smooth.*

It wasn't a total loss though. Money never stretched very far in the private security racket, and $775,000 would buy a lot of information and private jet miles.

Max tried to focus on the positives. Though Swift and his associates would know he was gunning for them now, it might work to his advantage. *They may reveal themselves inadvertently as they attempt to hide or come after me. And I got a really cool machine gun out of the deal. Sometimes, you can win by losing.*

Even botched missions had their rewards.

Max pulled his rented Toyota Tundra off of US 1 into a strip mall parking lot. After passing several typical shops—a nail salon, Dunkin Donuts, a pawn shop advertising top dollar for military gear and memorabilia—he parked in front of the last rented storefront, a bar named the Back Gate Grill. The name wasn't lost on him. Outside the back gate of just about every military base in the world stood at least one bar that catered to military personnel. Instead of referencing the bar by name, men headed out to drink would just say they were going "out the back gate." In this case, the savvy owner had made the term literal, though the Back Gate was several miles down US 1 from the back gate of Marine Corps Base Quantico.

Max's phone vibrated on the passenger seat. He read the text message from Ben Fisher, an FBI agent with whom he'd once served with in the Corps: *Held up at office. Leaving now be there in a few.* They had agreed it would be best to meet off base, away from the many thousands of probing ears. "Not that we have anything to hide," Fisher had joked when they set up the meeting. *Speak for yourself,* had been Max's only thought.

Max had a second reason to avoid Quantico. The place brought back too many memories, oddly enough, most of them good. He'd left his civilian life behind upon entering the front gate at Quantico in the late nineties. There, at OCS and then the Basic School, he was torn down and rebuilt into an officer of Marines. Marine Corps advertising billboards of the day had read "The Change is Forever" beneath the picture of the Marine in dress blues: calm, stern, and possessed of unshakeable bearing, the antithesis of the typically scatter-brained civilian. And it was certainly true. He left Quantico a better man, a motivated leader of men ready to confront and defeat any enemy unlucky enough to stand in his way.

But he had one huge problem with visiting the base—it always got him thinking *what if?* What if he'd been allowed to stay in the Marine Corps? He might be a lieutenant colonel waiting for wings or even retired. All contingent on not being killed, of course. Young infantry officers made their living dodging bullets, and he'd been assigned to an elite MARSOC unit—Marine Corps Forces Special Operations Command—when he'd parted ways from the corps.

I had a good career going, and it would only have gotten better.

Above all, had he remained a Marine he might still have a family.

But that hadn't happened. Instead, a major and a master gunnery sergeant framed him for the murder of his CO. In truth it was an accident, nothing to do with Max. Nevertheless, had his case gone to trial, Max would have been convicted and sentenced to death or life in prison. He could have handled that, but he couldn't have accepted the disgrace it would have brought upon his family.

At his most desperate hour, Max was summoned by Marklin, whom he had never met before. He offered Max a simple deal: join the CIA, be trained as an operative, and continue living his life as if nothing had happened. *Lies, all of it.* But Max accepted the deal, which wound up costing him all that he held dear.

Bitter over his ouster from the corps and disgruntled with his CIA field work, Max had been considered a volatile liability by his superiors. Before being torn apart by an alien creature, Max's former handler Peter Banner revealed that he arranged for Max's wife and son to be killed. Banner wanted to ensure the CIA had Max's complete loyalty and owed Max payback for torturing one of the man's covert contacts. The flawlessly executed hit was disguised as a drunk driving accident. That the police bought it was no surprise; it was painstakingly planned by a man with the alias Burt Jarvis, true name unknown, a legendary accident man who had since left the CIA for freelance work.

Since learning that his family hadn't died by accident, Max had been obsessed with finding Jarvis and his team. Three men had assisted Jarvis on the hit: Swift Carter; Scott Cleghorn, gunned down by Swift in Guyana; and a third man whose name Max still sought.

Max hoped Carter hadn't broken his arm while patting himself on the back for his not-so-daring escape. *Your days are numbered, double digits at the most.*

Once Max opened the smoked glass front door and stepped inside the bar, he realized he had visited it a few times before. *Yeah, I remember this place now.* Back then it had been called The Quatrefoil, a bit more upscale. The Back Gate Grill more resembled the stereotypical back gate bar: somewhat clean yet something of a dive. It had flags of the four services hanging on the walls amongst framed photos and unframed snapshots, mostly of Marines on operations in the Middle East, though Max also glimpsed a smattering of older photos from Vietnam and before.

They had agreed to meet at 1400, a dead hour in the food and beverage industry that would have afforded them privacy. Unfortunately, neither man had considered that certain units might have early liberty on Friday. About a dozen Marines, in service C uniforms of green trousers and short-sleeve khaki shirts with ribbons attached, monopolized three tables and a handful of barstools. Their ranks ranged from captain down to PFC. *Section party.* Max remembered them well. The first couple of rounds would be on the CO, who would then depart with his officers to avoid accusations of fraternization. After that, the staff NCOs might foot the bill for a couple more rounds before likewise bolting. The NCOs and nonrates would stay and drink their fill, some until last call.

Max didn't consider their presence a hindrance. He and Ben would be the last people on their minds, and he liked the raucous atmosphere as well. The jokes and camaraderie brought back some of his better memories of the Marine Corps.

He spied the waitress, a butter-faced brunette about his own age who compensated with a finely toned gym body. "Anywhere?" He motioned with a finger toward the tables.

"Anywhere's good, hon," she responded wearily from beneath a tray loaded with sweating longnecks.

Max took a seat near a table where four Marines played a hotly contested game of spades, while a couple more stood over their shoulders making snide comments. He ordered a bottle of Molson XXX, watched the game, and waited.

"Jesus, you'd think it was Friday around here," Ben Fisher said as he emerged from the press of Marines. A slimly built man of about 6'2", he cut a fine figure in his black government suit and teal tie. He had brown hair, a mouthful of even white teeth, and a natural charisma that made him popular with both ladies and gentlemen. Still living the single life, he showed no signs of settling down.

"How soon we forget," Max said as he came to his feet to shake hands.

"Whoa, nice mug!" Ben motioned to Max's face, which bore a few scabs from the splinters Imogene had dealt him.

"Woodchipper accident."

"Let me guess: I don't even want to know what you did to the woodchipper?"

Max shook his head. "Not a pretty sight."

Ben slapped him on the back and laughed heartily. "No machine can beat a Marine." He jerked a thumb over his shoulder. "Nice crowd. Hell, I like this unit. Why didn't you ever buy us drinks on an early Friday?"

"I did. Not that you slackers ever did anything to deserve it."

They sat and exchanged small talk. Ben worked out of the Bureau's Washington DC office but spent the last week commuting to Quantico on business. He didn't mention what sort of business, and Max knew better than to ask. In addition to several Marine Corps facilities, Quantico likewise played host to the FBI's training academy, hostage rescue team, and laboratory.

Max had known Ben for about fifteen years. He first met him in the corps, when Ben had been a stellar enlisted Marine in Max's rifle platoon. In recognition of his leadership and technical skill, Max recommended him for a meritorious promotion to corporal and eventually helped him to enter the Marine Corps enlisted commissioning program. Ben became a second lieutenant right about the time Max lost his Marine Corps career. After a couple of years as an officer, Ben resigned his commission to join the FBI. Max never expected Ben to repay him—he'd earned everything Max had assisted him with—but hopefully their history would buy him a favor right now when he really needed it.

"You doing lunch, Max?"

"Nah, I ate already. You eat at odd hours."

"Didn't have a choice today. Goddamn mess at the office, shit really hit the fan. Lucky I got out of there when I did." He flagged down the waitress and ordered a shit-ton of food: pickle chips, a bacon double cheeseburger, and fries. "Think we need a pitcher of beer too, doll," he added with a smile, eliciting one in return from the jaded waitress.

"Hope you're buying," Max said after her departure.

"Of course. Somebody around here has to support the CIA."

"Oh, now you're gettin' nasty." Though Max had left the Agency behind years ago, Ben and his other friends would never allow him to forget whom he'd served. *Not that the Bureau is any better.*

They spent the better part of an hour reminiscing and drinking beer. By the time they started their second pitcher, the unit's staff and officers had predictably departed, leaving the lower ranks to freely carouse. Ben had polished off the mountain of greasy food with no aid whatsoever from Max, who decided to get to business before their slight buzzes turned into something much dizzier. He had a feeling they might be in for a late night and, oddly enough, found himself in the mood for just that.

Fuck it; it's been a rough week.

Ben seemed to read his mind. "I'm heading back to DC after this. You up to hit the town later? I'll let you be my wingman."

Max laughed. "Bullshit. You can be mine."

"Your Cruise to my Kilmer. Let the panties hit the floor!"

"We might be able to splash a couple. But first we need to discuss some heavier shit."

"I agree. After you, I insist."

Max didn't like the sound of that. He hadn't expected to receive a reciprocal load of heavy shit. "I need a lead on someone. You familiar with the name Henry Carter? Goes by the nickname of Swift?"

Ben shook his head. "Doesn't ring a bell."

"He's former Agency, became a contractor after that. We have a history, you might say, and it isn't exactly rosy."

"Not wingman material?"

"Not at all. He couldn't get laid in a barnyard." *Especially now.*

"Ouch! What do you need this guy for? Something work related?"

"Something like that."

Ben gave him a patronizing stare while attempting to suppress his amusement. "Now, Max, it would be unethical for me to assist you in such matters. As you know, the Bureau does not condone nor take part in feuds, vigilantism—"

"Did I mention he's former CIA? I figured you'd be interested on that fact alone."

Ben laughed, poured more beer. "We harbor no grudges toward our sister agencies. Wherever did you get an idea like that?"

Max shrugged. "Too much television?"

Ben shot a finger gun at him. "Exactly..." He then cracked up laughing, and Max wondered if he'd waited a few rounds too long to get to business. The beer appeared to be working on Ben already. But then he at least managed to *look* serious. "Tell you what, Max, give me what you have on the guy, and I'll see what I can do."

"Thanks, buddy, I really—"

"In return for a favor, of course. One hand washes the other... well, you know."

Max suppressed a sigh. *Of course.* "All too well. Shoot."

Ben leaned over the table, taking care for the first time that no one hear their conversation. "I'm working hand-in-hand with the lab at Quantico on a very crucial assignment, highest priority in the Bureau. It's called Operation Thinker, though we just call it The Thinker."

"Objective?"

"We're after something too, only it's not a person. Help me procure it, and I'll dig up all I can on the current whereabouts of your Mr. Carter. If not, our business ends here. But we party tonight nevertheless." He raised his glass in salute, then downed the dregs of his beer.

Max might have walked out at this point, so often had he been tempted with broken promises uttered by forked tongues. He'd definitely developed his share of trust issues, which multiplied each time he sought information on his family's killers. Ben had never given Max a reason to distrust him, but government work could corrupt even a man of probity. Max could only hope the Bureau hadn't gotten too deep into Ben's head. At the present time, he had few other options for help.

"I might be open to that," Max said. "But why would you even think of bringing me in on this operation? I haven't had an active security clearance in years."

Ben appeared troubled for the first time. "Because I think there's a mole in the Bureau, possibly several. I need someone from the outside, someone I trust. Accept, and we'll each go about our missions. I'll start searching for your boy Carter first thing Monday morning."

After a few moments of rumination, Max said, "Deal. Now tell me what you suits are after."

Looking very pleased with himself, Ben flashed a smile. *If you think you're getting something for nothing, you're sorely mistaken.* Even with the Bureau's resources, Swift would be quite difficult to locate.

Ben leaned even closer so he could be heard over a drunk Marine at the spades table shouting, *Bullshit! You reneged!* "What we're after is called Nexus."

Nexus? Max upended his glass and waited to hear more.

5

Max had learned of Swift's presence on team Jarvis almost immediately after the Guyana mission; unfortunately, he hadn't been able to hunt him down right away due to many grievous injuries he'd sustained on the mission, particularly a gunshot wound to the shoulder that required several months of intense physical therapy to heal and recondition. Those months had crept past as he constantly obsessed over capturing Carter and learning the identities of the others behind the crime. Home life, doctors' visits, and an intense daily routine of working out and shooting nearly drove him mad as he waited and healed, eager to get on the road and continue his quest, his cyber searches for leads turning up nothing. When the time arrived to go after Swift, he left home determined and prepared, certain of taking down Carter as a steppingstone to locating the others.

His subsequent failure still needled him as he raised the overhead door of the climate-controlled storage unit where he'd deposited his gear. Though he owned a luxurious home in Henderson, Nevada, just outside Las Vegas, Max had long ago grown accustomed to living in hotels and keeping his valuables in storage lockers. After his long period of recuperation, road life was the panacea he required to truly complete his recovery.

But Max found his enthusiasm waning in the wake of the Florida debacle. *Working for promises again…* It had become an old and familiar theme, but at least the other missions provided cash compensation, if not the names he sought. He shook off the thought and turned to his gear. His private jet flight to San Francisco departed at 1600, three hours from now. If he must lament, it would be more prudent to do so on the plane.

He'd seen nothing of Ben that morning. His wingman had scored; Max fell asleep on his couch listening to the creaking of bedsprings through the wall, accompanied by grunts and groans of pleasure. Max, who didn't really go for looser sorts of women, had settled for a bit of second-base action and the phone number of an attractive yet generic blond about ten years his junior, which was fine by him. He'd wound up going on a mission with the last woman he picked up in a dance club, a CIA snake named Juno Rey, who tried to murder him a few days later in North Korea. Last night was a different situation, not lethal in the slightest, but it paid to be picky about whom one slept with.

Ben hadn't elaborated much regarding Nexus, opting instead to provide Max with a computer file on a flash drive that explained everything… or, more likely, only what Ben wished him to know. After departing Ben's place that morning with a mild hangover, he returned to his hotel to review the file on his laptop before checking out, reading it over four times until he memorized all of the principal details.

Nexus was an artificial intelligence program, allegedly the most advanced ever created, able to penetrate the security firewalls of any computer system in the world and hijack their operating systems. The US government coveted the program strictly for security reasons, or so they claimed. *Oh sure, they would never use it to hack the computer systems of other governments.* But turnabout was fair play, he supposed, if one believed the claims that China and Russia were constantly hacking in to mine data from the US government. In the intelligence community, one either kept pace with the enemy or fell victim to its attacks.

As he began loading his 40-liter backpack with gear—starting with several boxes each of .45 and .380 ammunition, along with silencers and extra magazines for the two pistols—he again broke down the information on Dr. Daniel Farber, creator of Nexus. A wealthy Israeli national, forty years old and a widower, Farber had been educated at prestigious institutions abroad and in the United States. He'd earned dual doctorates in computer science and robotics from MIT, after which he returned to Israel to forge his career in AI.

Nexus, Farber's ultimate brainchild, could well be his last. After word of Nexus leaked to the intelligence community, interests from around the world sought to procure it. Harassed and threatened, Farber departed Israel. After a harrowing journey across the world he arrived in America, the only place where he might find succor. Of course, Farber would be forced to surrender Nexus to his saviors, the FBI, if they could get him to a safehouse located outside DC.

Though the file mentioned nothing about the CIA or Mossad, Max knew they would be after Nexus as well. In fact, with Farber now in America, CIA agents would likely pose the greatest threat to him reaching the safehouse.

That's where I come in.

FBI special agents Donald Wagner and Margaret Leet had been tasked with getting Farber from the West Coast to DC. Unfortunately, their journey went horribly wrong before it even started, when Wagner, the veteran agent of the two, was gunned down in the bathroom at Los Angeles Union Station by an unidentified man trying to steal Nexus. The hostile operative failed to secure the plans, but now only Leet stood between Farber and those scheming to steal his creation.

Ben, Leet's DC contact and the man charged with securing Nexus for the Bureau, feared a mole in the organization and was reluctant to assign another agent to assist Leet. The fewer insiders who knew of Nexus, the better. Thus he'd called in Max to help her deliver Nexus and Dr. Farber.

These were the official facts. But Ben had added his own addendum to the file, regarding Special Agent Leet. Twenty-eight years old, she had been with the Bureau for only three years and, in addition to being inexperienced and outgunned, Ben believed that she had been romantically involved with her deceased partner, Wagner. Max understood his concerns, having lost a few romantic interests on missions himself. She might be rattled and unstable over her partner's death. Even if Leet had kept herself together, it sounded like she could use all the help she could get.

Max sorted his gear in earnest as time grew shorter. *If nothing else, this will be a change of pace.* For this rare mission into the civilian world, Max would be leaving his full combat load behind. No need for a heavy-duty plate carrier, ballistic helmet, rifle, or tactical suits in several environmental patterns. He did pack suits in both black and urban camouflage, just in case, along with a pair of night vision goggles he would carry in his luggage.

Knowing he might be forced to fly commercial in the following days, Max was hesitant to pack heavier firepower. Flying with two legal pistols these days proved difficult enough; a submachine gun could land him in jail. Yet his instincts screamed at him to err on the side of caution, even if he had to leave the weapon behind in storage to get on a plane.

His HK MP-7 had always served well as a backup weapon on combat missions, but he chose instead to bring a new addition to his arsenal—a Springfield Armory Saint chambered in 5.56mm, a compact, cutting-edge, AR-15-style pistol that he'd yet to wield under fire. It had an EOTech holographic red dot sight, a custom-built suppressor, and a thirty-round magazine clamped to a second mag for rapid reload. The Saint was only slightly larger than his MP-7, and the larger round it carried would allow him to engage targets at both close and long range. Max put the Saint and two sets of attached magazines into the backpack along with some spare ammunition and batteries.

Even knives could present a problem while traveling. He already wore his Boker in an ankle sheath. His Ka-Bar might be overkill on this mission, yet he found himself packing it anyway. *Might come in handy. I can wear it at the small of my back under a sport jacket if need be.*

As in Florida, non-lethal weapons could prove crucial to success, as gunplay tended to be frowned upon in the civilian world, sure to bring down the law on them in a hurry. He found a can of pepper spray and a stun gun that was, alas, not as powerful as the baton he'd lost in Florida, but it might do in a pinch. He had wanted to find a Taser, preferably an X26, but neither of the two gun shops he hit had them in stock. He made a mental note to acquire one whenever he got back home. He also packed the same low-vis plate carrier he'd worn to Swift's house and planned on living in it for the next few days.

What am I missing? He paused and thought for a moment. *Comm gear.* He found the earpiece radio he'd purchased a while back for working in the civilian world. Though it was a few years old now, he figured it would synch to whatever frequency Leet normally used. *If not, I hope she has a spare I can borrow.*

His eyes lit on the handheld, waterproof GPS unit he'd never returned to the CIA after his mission to North Korea. He packed it as a fail-safe in case they got lost in the middle of nowhere.

He decided to bring $25,000 for miscellaneous expenses, drawn from Swift's safe. Ben could provide no upfront funds for expenses since the mission was off the FBI's books for the moment, but he'd promised to reimburse Max when Farber was delivered. Leet, being a special agent, would have her own expense account. Between them, he didn't envision running out of funds.

He looked over the remaining items to ensure he hadn't forgotten anything. "That should about do it." He sealed the backpack and stepped out of the locker.

Max took one last glimpse at what he was leaving behind as he pulled down the door: MG34, antique flintlock pistol, nearly all of his personal weapons and field gear, and $750,000 in cash. This storage facility advertised as the most secure in the DC metro area; the place even had armed security. He didn't sweat having his possessions stolen, but he did wonder what would happen if he never returned. He'd harbored such ominous forebodings at the beginning of missions since his days in the corps as a married man, when his death would have devastated his family. That, at least, he no longer worried about, his only benefit as a widower, yet thoughts of death still haunted him every time he headed off to work.

You won't be missed. Some collector cleans up, I suppose. He thought of the TV show where abandoned storage lockers were auctioned to the highest bidder. For an investment of a few thousand dollars, some lucky schnook might retire in style to the high life.

It won't come to that, he assured himself as he departed. *It's not time. I have too much left to do.* These thoughts awakened others, eventually conjuring one of the most unreliable words in the English language: destiny. *I'll have their names and, after that, their heads.* He wouldn't let a few stooges trying to steal a computer program stand in his way. For the love he still bore his family, he would fulfill his destiny.

My final mission. And after their heads roll, then I can die.

If hangovers could truly be compared to dog bites, then Max had merely been nipped by a chihuahua. He considered himself lucky. If he'd kept up with Ben, he would have been mauled by a pit bull. As it stood, his bite would require nothing more than a double Maker's Mark, which he poured over a couple of rocks at the bar in the rear of the private jet's cabin. He required no stewardess when flying alone; such pretensions were for people with bottomless pockets and towering egos. Merely avoiding commercial air travel, with its seat-kicking children and lengthy security lines, was good enough for him. He also enjoyed the added benefit of privacy.

He returned to his seat, a throne of leather, chrome, and teakwood, and settled down to sip his whisky, listening to the muted whine of jet engines laboring out in the freezing atmosphere. In addition to taming the dog, he hoped the bourbon might lull him to sleep. He had almost six hours to kill before arrival in San Francisco, and though he didn't feel the slightest bit tired, he had to consider the three-hour jetlag. He needed to be completely alert from the moment he touched down. The prescription sleeping pills in his pack were not an option at the moment, too strong for a nap of only a few hours, their sole purpose to knock him senseless so that he might sleep an entire night free from PTSD dreams. Hopefully the whisky would suffice to help the dead stay dead and the past stay past.

He faced an empty leather chair as wide and luxurious as his own. *It's better this way.* In past missions, he departed with traveling companions who hadn't lived to catch the return flight. *They knew the dangers or claimed to at any rate.* His last mercenary team, hardened veterans of both the military and government agencies, certainly knew. Max left them all in Alaska, some on the spacecraft and others on the frozen earth. All physical traces of them had disappeared when the ship exploded in a powerful nuclear fireball.

His last traveling companion, an investigative reporter named Iris Keller who went by the nickname Heat, might have stayed home if she'd truly known her chances of survival. Martyrdom, for all its allure to idealistic fools, held little appeal to her during the final hours of her life, which she had spent on the run from Gideon Wilde's rented soldiers and reptilian creations. *Dying in the name of truth, as if anyone gives a screaming shit about that. Could anything have been more wasteful?*

"Yeah, living a lie, silly," answered an amused female sitting in the seat opposite him. Heavily tattooed, she sipped a double martini and beamed at him, the muted cabin lighting dancing off her numerous piercings and neon-blue hair. "But I don't live that way, remember?" Heat raised her glass in salute and declared, "I am the Voltaire of our time!"

"And you still died," Max said.

She laughed, a ghostly tinkling of wind chimes. "Whatever gave you that idea?"

With a start, Max noticed the coins covering her eyes, a pair of freshly minted Morgan silver dollars, Lady Liberty facing outward.

"I'm not going anywhere," Heat continued. "I'll always be with you." Max couldn't help but stare at the coins as she leaned in closer and seductively whispered, "Isn't that what you want?"

No, I don't. Now fucking go away! He knew what was happening, where he really was. *Wake up! Get out of this before it's—*

The blackness behind his closed eyelids turned a brilliant vermilion. He opened his eyes on a tropical vista of endless azure sky above a deep cobalt sea, a silhouette of gray coastline far in the distance. The only thing missing from this paradise was a beautiful woman to share it with, though he realized in the next instant that he'd brought one along when he looked down and saw Heat—the top of her bobbing head, anyway, her hair now dyed jet black—as she sucked vigorously on his cock, which tingled and threatened to explode at any moment.

She broke off in the middle of her business to gaze up at him with her silver dollar eyes. "You're right, Max. It's all part of the game." She took him in her mouth once more and resumed as a metallic squawking assaulted Max's ears. He didn't give a shit about the noise, however, even as it intensified—all of his nerves seemed to radiate from his crotch.

The trombone bleats of gibberish continued; the blow job did not. Max opened his eyes, looked down as the noise filled his head with a deafening racket that churned his brain.

Pleasure turned to pain in a heartbeat, when he saw the red smear on the fly of his swimming trunks and noticed the blood pissing from the stump of his cock. All of the injuries he'd ever sustained—combined—couldn't match his pain in that moment. He cried out in agony and fright, yet made not a sound, his vocal cords brittle, paralyzed, dry rotted.

Even as he silently screamed, he looked down upon Heat, whose black hair had grown long and lustrous, shining with healthy radiance and the gleam of fresh blood. She gazed upward, no longer

Heat, but CIA operative Juno Rey, who chewed loudly and smacked her lips as she merrily munched on the remnants of his member like the ghoul that she was. She gulped down the remainder of his manhood with a strained swallow, then said with a smile, "It's only business, Max." Narrow vertical slits slashed her golden eyes, so much like those of the serpents he'd encountered at Swift's house.

Max tried to push her away, only to find that his limbs had grown rigid and immobile. The squawking grew frantic and threatening, a raucous crescendo crashing about in his skull that quickly eclipsed all other sounds.

The nonsensical noise then coalesced into spoken words that Max didn't wish to hear. He'd left sun and sea behind, and now stood in the kitchen of his old house near Minneapolis. "We lived here," he said aloud, bewildered.

"What the fuck are you talking about?" demanded his wife, Janet.

Max looked upon her in relief. He not only had his cock back, but also his wife to use it on. He couldn't fucking wait. Sure, she'd gained a few pounds since David had come along, yet it hadn't wrecked her womanly shape, that perfect hourglass he'd fallen for way back in college. If anything, the slight amount of extra meat on her bones enhanced her figure. She hadn't changed a bit since the last time he'd seen her, still fair-skinned and brunette, with brown—*No, look again.* Her eyes were no longer brown, but rather two marbles of gleaming onyx with not a white to be seen.

"I'm waiting, Max." She impatiently tapped her foot as she leaned against the countertop.

"We live here!" Max responded. *No past tense about it!* As for her eyes, well, he would worry about that later.

"No shit, really?" She laughed at him. "Correction, David and I live here. You live in a war zone somewhere in the Third World."

Reason with her. Tell her the truth! Janet had always been level-headed until… "Not for much longer. I had it out with Banner the other day, told him I've had enough of this shit. He says he'll put me on an anti-terrorism team here in the states. I'll never be far—"

"You'll still be gone all the time! New York or New Guinea, what's the fucking difference? David still doesn't get a father, and I still don't get a husband."

"Look, you've got to believe—" He cut off his words when he noticed her sobbing.

"I… I'd like to believe that you'll be here. But it's always a lie. You *said* you'd take David to the park last week after school. But where were you when the school bus showed up?"

"You know where I was."

"Venezuela! Where else would my globe-trotting, adrenaline-junkie husband be? Got to go where the action is, right? Why work a normal job like the rest of humanity? You're happier shooting people for a living than you are with your own family. We're supposed to be what you fight for, but you'd rather just fight."

Max opened his mouth to protest yet uttered no words, his mind a blank slate but for two disturbing thoughts: *Is she right? Is that true?*

"We're just not good enough for you, I guess. So how many other women have you fucked during your crucial government missions?" She asked in the offhanded tone of a stranger inquiring about the weather.

"Never!" Max shouted. "I would never do that to you, Janet; I love you!"

She quieted, stared him down. Her black eyes seemed bottomless, twin portals to the netherworld. "Then prove it, prove that we come first. Call Banner right now, tell him you're sitting this one out."

"Janet, I can't do that, not yet, but soon enough—"

"Then why are you still here? You have to go on another mission. By all means, don't let us hold you back!"

"All right, I'm staying," Max announced, iron in his voice. "You're right, I can't go this time."

"Really? And what the hell's stopping you? Surely not us?"

"It is you. If I leave, you'll both be dead when I come home." He knew this to be true, only he didn't know how he'd acquired such knowledge.

Her laughter began haltingly, a couple of snorts that developed into a chuckle that soon morphed into a full-blown fit of guffawing.

Max could take no more. He crossed the kitchen in two long strides, seized Janet by the arms and shook her. "Stop it! I know—"

"And who's going to kill us, Max?" She laughed some more. "Is it Burt Jarvis? Wait, why am I asking you? Ten years later and you still don't know who fucking killed us! Professor Plum, Miss Scarlet…? It's all too much for you. You never did see the big picture."

"'Cause he's fucking worthless!" shouted a voice from behind him. *Oh, hell no!* That rasping, nicotine-ravaged voice he'd neither hoped nor expected to hear ever again added, "Just like his limp-dicked father!"

Max rounded on his mother, not with the intention of confronting her, but rather to kill her. She stood there for the taking, just as he remembered her: high hair bleached blond and reeking of hairspray, pancake makeup, whorish turquoise eye shadow, sneering around a cigarette burning between pink lips. She held a wine cooler, of course, one of the dozen or so she drank every day.

He noticed all of this in an instant as he pivoted and threw a right with every ounce of power and momentum he could muster. *Some dreams do come true!* His fist caught her square in the face. Sparks of burning tobacco showered the kitchen like a fireworks display. The satisfaction he felt when he knocked out her teeth and split her nose in half couldn't be measured. This instant of revenge had a *je na sais quoi* all its own.

Blood fountained into the air, lots of it, and all of it black, devouring all light as it covered the floor, the walls, Janet, the entire world in stygian ink…

Max treaded slowly and cautiously through pitch blackness. Despite the all-consuming dark, he felt somewhat at home in his plate carrier and helmet, a full combat load on his back, his trusty HK416 in his gloved hands. He switched on the flashlight mounted on his rifle. The white LED beam traveled unimpeded into infinity, lighting nothing in any direction, even when he pointed it at his feet. *Nothing there.* But he had feet, even if he couldn't see them, and knew that he walked on something other than ether. His footfalls rang against a hard surface, less metallic than steel yet more resonant than wood.

The sound gave it away. *I'm on the spaceship.*

Dull lights of amber and orange, the glow of alien electronics, gradually illuminated the area and confirmed his suspicions. *The reactor control room.*

He saw her, back turned to him as she opened a door and stepped into the airlock to access the reactor. His breath caught in his throat as he watched her. *So beautiful…* Men had fought wars over lesser women than the one who called herself Dr. Alexis Rogers, who was in every sense—body, mind, origin—out of this world. Angel or alien, he needed her now.

And now she was leaving him behind again. "I hope our paths cross again in another life," she said before slamming the door shut.

"Wait!" Max shouted, running the few steps to the airlock door. "I'm coming with you!" He threw open the door, passed into the airlock, and peered through the window on the second door. Already far away, she was busy with the holographic computer controls on one of the reactor towers, her brown ponytail beginning to curl and smoke from the intense heat in the reactor room, her skin turning red and starting to fissure.

Max closed his eyes for a moment, wiped them clean, and waited a moment before trying to peer into the intense brightness again. She'd moved out of sight by that time. *What? Where is she? Is the energy too much, even for her?*

A shadow moved in front of the door, blocking out the light. His vision went black; his eyes couldn't adjust fast enough. He blinked, rubbed his eyes, tried again to see. With great difficulty he identified her face, features shaded by the brilliant light now pouring from the reactor. She had her hands pressed against the glass. Her flesh had cracked, but her eyes were still brown, still penetrating. He could feel the reactor's heat even through the barrier. She smiled at him.

"I'll always be with you, Max," she said, her voice still bewitching and mellifluous.

He then watched in dumbstruck horror as she burst into flames; hair, clothes, skin, all gone in a blink, leaving behind only a grinning, burning skeleton.

"We all will!" she uttered, a voice and a promise from hell. She then burst through the window, showering him with glass shards and exposing him to blast-furnace heat.

Max's scream cut off abruptly when she wrapped fiery fingers around his throat and squeezed...

He awoke, choking in his seat. His drink had slipped from his hand to spill on the floor. But he recovered quickly, perhaps the only advantage of suffering regular and recurring nightmares. At least he could accept them for what they were when he awoke to the real world. But he knew he wouldn't be falling asleep again anytime soon. He checked his watch: 1703. *Great. Only five more hours to kill.*

Resigned to remaining awake, he opened his laptop to review

Ben's file once more. Instead he found himself staring at the screen, his thoughts anxious and unsettled. He spent most of the next few hours pacing the cabin, until the pilot announced their final approach into San Francisco.

* * *

Max entered the wi-fi café in downtown San Francisco where he was to meet Special Agent Leet, who had chosen the busy rendezvous point for safety reasons. When on the run, it was best to stay with the herd, even if they didn't have your back. Dozens of possible witnesses could deter all but the most intrepid attackers.

Laden with over fifty pounds of clothing, weapons, and gear in the large pack on his back, he almost felt like he'd stepped off on another merc mission in the middle of nowhere. Adopting the guise of a tourist backpacker transiting the Pacific Coast Trail, he wore a baggy, water-repellent, softshell jacket to conceal the low-vis plate carrier and the Glock 21 holstered on his hip. The plate carrier held two spare magazines for all three of his weapons and a blow-out first aid kit, all accessible at a moment's notice. Loose cargo pants and a pair of high-end hiking shoes completed his getup.

The collective aromas of several different coffee varieties socked him in his olfactory. He'd never been a coffee drinker, couldn't stand the taste of it. But Janet had been a devoted drinker of swamp water, and during his married years he came to appreciate boiling coffee as a smell of home, the only true home he'd ever known. It had become an annoying stench since losing her however.

Find Leet and get this over with.

He expected to spot her easily amongst the patrons; she would be the only one paying any attention to her surroundings. With the exception of one filthy man with a three-foot ponytail who sat reading a book—perhaps an original hippie; he was old enough—the customers stared obliviously at their electronic devices, ignoring even their companions across the tables. Max shook his head. *Why even leave the house?* Oddly enough, he probably shared more in common with the hippie than with anyone else in the place. They might have had a stimulating dialogue regarding the machinations of the military-industrial complex. *Some other time perhaps.*

He didn't notice her until she made herself known by signaling with a raised index finger. *No wonder, she's changed her appearance.* Ben's file included three pictures of Leet: one, a posed official photo for her FBI identification badge, and two candid shots. In all three, she wore the ubiquitous dark power suit of a female federal agent and had shoulder-length brown hair. The present Leet wore a faded brown leather jacket, tight faded jeans, and a pair of leather equestrian boots with too many brass buckles. She'd likewise dyed her hair jet black and cut it maybe too short. She looked a lot like Heat, minus several pounds of piercings and a couple quarts of ink. But the resemblance ended there. Heat had been several inches shorter, thin and rather stringy. Leet was tall—Max figured she stood 5'9" or so—and had the body of an avid gym rat. Not female bodybuilder big but pretty solid nonetheless.

Looks like she could handle herself in a fight. That was good; he'd been worried about having to babysit her as well as Farber.

Max set his pack on the floor and sat down across from her. Introductions were waived as unnecessary. "Nice getup," Max said. "Took me a minute to spot you."

"It won't fool anyone for very long," she responded, hazel eyes darting to the door as a young couple entered, each mesmerized by their glowing phone screen.

"Sometimes you only need a few seconds. Where's your package?"

She appeared amused, though nervously so. "You tell me."

Max scanned the café for Farber, whom he'd likewise reviewed photos of. It took him longer than a minute to find him, or a man who *might* be Farber, sitting at a table about halfway to the door, where Leet could easily observe him as he stared into a tablet, occasionally touching the screen as he read. His hair had been bleached from dark brown to light, and he wore a canvas outdoor hat with a wide brim that shaded his features. His expensive eyeglasses were the only giveaway, the same pair he wore in the photographs.

Across from him sat a boy, his back to Max, who wore a black baseball cap over black hair cropped very short, almost shaved off. Scowling, Max turned back to Leet. "Why did you seat a kid with him? That boy's in danger."

"That boy is part of the package, as in package deal."

"What?"

She leaned closer and whispered, "That's Farber's son, Shai."

Are you fucking kidding me? "Ben didn't mention anything about a kid."

"I wonder why? Maybe he thought you might have balked at his offer."

After a moment of disgusted pondering on how federal agents tended to dissemble regarding crucial details, Max said, "He would have been wrong, but it's spilled milk now." *Only an unexpected catch, no mission is complete without at least one. But why would Farber drag his son into this kind of danger? Kidnapping threats?* The boy's presence would certainly complicate things. "You need to fill me in on any other details Ben might have accidentally left out."

"Not here, not now." She drained the last of her coffee in one swallow. "We're going to the restrooms. Leave the door unlocked; they'll meet you in there. Wait three minutes, then take them out the rear door to the alley. I have an Uber waiting for us."

"Understood."

They headed to the johns, located down a short hallway at the rear of the café. A steel door at the end of the hallway barred access to the alley, its red push bar reading **Emergency Exit Only! Alarm Will Sound!** *Then I hope she disabled it.*

They entered their respective bathrooms. Max considered breaking out the Saint for the trip to the car yet decided against it. Though he could conceal it easily enough beneath the windbreaker, it was best left in his pack for now, especially in gun-shy San Francisco. The Glock which had served him well on so many missions would suffice.

The door opened about thirty seconds later, admitting Daniel Farber and his son. Farber tightly clutched a metal briefcase in one hand, which Max assumed held the Nexus software. The day packs they wore likely contained whatever remained of their worldly possessions. He pegged the boy, who clutched a ratty stuffed rabbit in his left hand, at about eight to ten years old.

Emotional turmoil rose immediately in his gut. He thought of David, who had died at that age, as well as other children he'd encountered in warzones throughout his career. Since joining the Marine Corps years before, his attitude on war had always been to accept it for the insanity it was, with the exception of children, none of whom should ever have had to endure such brutality and privation. Civilian adults could usually get out of the way if they really wanted to; children rarely had that option.

Max and Farber introduced themselves and shook hands. "Mr. Ahlgren," Farber said. "It is a pleasure. I hope you can help us."

Max noted his slow and careful manner of speech, found it rather odd for a man so brilliant. *Maybe foreign languages aren't his thing. They're certainly not mine.* "We'll get you where you need to be." He turned his attention downward to the boy, offered his hand and realized he'd already forgotten the kid's name. "I'm Max; it's nice to meet you."

The boy only stared at him with an uncertain look of wonder.

"Remember your manners, Shai," Farber said. He didn't patronize the boy or express disapproval but said it in a manner appropriate for a father teaching a son. "Mr. Ahlgren is going to help us."

Shai nodded, reached up, and shook Max's hand, though he remained silent. *He'll require careful observation.* Having been raised by a genius, Shai might be the precocious and inquisitive type, likely to wander off and examine whatever caught his fancy. David had certainly been that sort. *And I'm damn far from being a genius.*

"Good grip there, pal," Max said, smiling. "You've got a cool name. I've never heard it before."

The corners of Shai's mouth rose slightly, probably the closest thing to a smile the kid had left in him. *He's been chased across the world. Poor kid's probably in shellshock.* "It means *gift* in Hebrew," Shai bashfully informed him.

Max nodded. "I like it." He patted Shai on the shoulder. "And both of you need to call me Max. We're family for the next few days."

"My apologies, Max," Farber said.

"Not necessary." He checked his watch. "We need to go now. Stay right behind me and do exactly what I say. There's a car waiting for us out back."

Not waiting for acknowledgement, Max opened the door and checked the hallway. Empty. He stepped into the hall and remembered how much he hated jobs like this. No one in the café appeared threatening, yet he remained wary of taking his eyes off Daniel and Shai. *Leet must have been shitting eggrolls these past few days.* That she'd kept them alive on her own testified to her skill and planning. For an inexperienced agent, she seemed to be on top of things.

No alarm sounded as they exited into the alley where Leet awaited them. Max didn't like the dark alley. Dumpsters, trash cans, and miscellaneous junk lined the dingy walls of narrow brick. *Too many hiding spots.* He had to consider the vertical as well as the horizontal—the dozens of windows and fire escapes overhead where attackers might be lurking.

"Car's down there." Leet pointed to a vehicle about a hundred feet down the alley, near the last couple of dumpsters and close to a street. "He wouldn't pull all the way in here."

Max understood why; bits of trash and broken glass littered the pavement amongst potholes the depth of atomic test craters. Suddenly he regretted leaving the Saint in his backpack, but Leet had made it sound as if the car was parked outside the doorway. *She needs to be more specific in the future.* "Let's do it fast, then," he said, taking the lead. The Farbers walked between them, with Leet keeping eyes out in the rear.

As he quickly stepped to the car, a blue Nissan Xterra about ten years old, Max tried to scrutinize every shadow. A part of his conscience chided him for being paranoid, while the rest of it applauded his cautious prudence, even though he hadn't the time for a more thorough examination. The abundance of earthbound hiding spots confined Max's overhead surveillance to brief glances.

They reached the SUV soon enough, which sat idling as the driver waited, no doubt a violation in the green city of San Francisco. Max stowed his pack in the rear as the Farbers piled into the back seat. Leet knew where they were headed; still Max needed to ride shotgun. No way could he fit in the back seat with Daniel and Shai.

Leet and Max jumped in simultaneously and closed their doors. "Let's go," Leet said.

The vehicle did not move. The driver, a Sikh wearing a black turban, appeared to have fallen asleep while waiting.

"Wake up!" Max ordered, shaking him violently by the shoulder. Only then did he notice the dark blotches on the driver's face, and as his head lolled over and thumped the driver's side window, Max saw the purple ligature marks on his neck.

Tearing his attention from the dead driver, Max saw two men step around corners of buildings to block the alley: one was dressed like a businessman in a dark suit, the other like a derelict wearing a filthy overcoat that hung past his knees.

"Get down!" Max shouted, drawing his Glock.

His choice became obvious as they reached for concealed weapons. The bum in the overcoat would be toting the real firepower. Assuming they wore body armor, Max aimed for the guy's head through the windshield. He squeezed off a shot as the bum brought up a silenced submachine gun from within the folds of his overcoat. The windshield exploded into a cloudy mosaic of blue-green safety glass, minus a .45 caliber hole dead center, and he couldn't see if he'd taken out the bum.

He ducked behind the dashboard as rounds started flying through the windshield, rapid shots from a silenced semi-auto that showered the cabin with pebbles of glass. The snap of bullets striking the car and flying overhead was nearly deafening. Pandemonium erupted in the back seat, Farber yelling in panic, Leet shouting at them to stay down.

Max leaned over, found the driver's side door handle, and pulled. The Sikh, who'd already been leaning in that direction, tumbled from the SUV to the cracked pavement as more trouble literally descended on them. With a resounding metallic boom, an enemy operative landed atop a dumpster on the passenger side of the vehicle. A louder boom sounded in the next instant when yet another crashed down on the roof of the Xterra, shaking the car.

Leet's pistol, the only non-silenced weapon in the fight, popped twice, shattering one of the rear windows. A scream came from outside as Max attempted to take the wheel without exposing himself to enemy gunfire. "Go, go!" she shouted.

I'm fucking trying! But bullets kept flying over his head, and minus that vital appendage, they wouldn't be going anywhere. When the other rear window shattered, Max knew he had to risk it. He slid over the console trying to contort his 6'4" frame behind the wheel. Upholstery stuffing exploded from the driver's seat when a bullet with his name on it struck the headrest.

Still not fully in the driver's seat, Max shifted into drive, found the gas with his right foot, and stomped it, finally exposing himself above the steering wheel. Fortunately, the enemy fire had completely destroyed the windshield, allowing him a clear view. He'd timed his move just right, the enemy in the suit reloading his pistol. Tires smoked and wailed as Max laid down rubber, bound for the street.

But there would be a slight detour involved. The suited man put his next shot past Max's ear in a final attempt to stop him. *Wrong answer.* Wrenching the wheel hard right, Max clipped him as he dove for cover behind the last dumpster. *Dammit!* The guy wouldn't be getting up anytime soon, but he'd survived the vehicular assault. Metal screeched and sparks flew when the passenger side raked the brick building, but Max got the SUV back on keel and shot out of the alley, almost t-boning another car as he swerved into the street.

Aware of the man clinging to the roof, which featured a luggage rack for his comfort and convenience, Max cut a sharp left onto the street amidst bleating horns and screeching tires of cars braking or fleeing from his path. The Xterra proved to be a surprisingly powerful SUV, difficult to control as he tried to straighten her out. He sideswiped a Prius and sent it careening into the roll-down metal door safeguarding the storefront of a closed business.

Leet fired twice through the roof, the rounds deafening in the enclosed space, eliciting more frantic shouts from Daniel, this time in a language Max guessed to be Hebrew. *Fuck, he's still up there.* With the Xterra now under his control, Max floored it and steered into the oncoming lane to pass several cars sitting at a red light, almost running head-on into a car turning onto the street. He slowed as he passed the sitting cars, banged a right, and charged down a steep hill. He didn't even want to look at the speedometer as he moved into the oncoming lane to pass a car creeping downgrade, narrowly avoiding a streetcar laboring uphill.

Leet was on her own in the back seat. Max couldn't possibly know what she was doing, but it sounded as if she were grappling with the man's gun arm as he shoved his pistol through the window.

You're about done, pal. Max gunned the engine as the traffic light ahead turned from yellow to red. Cars began crossing the intersection. "Shit! Hang on!" Somehow, timing remained on his side as he shot the gap between two crossing cars, the SUV leveling off for an instant before catching air on the downhill side of the intersection.

Max heard a silenced shot from the rear as they sailed through thin air. Farber shrieked. The Xterra bucked when its wheels returned to pavement, the steering wheel animated in Max's hands as the top-heavy SUV shimmied violently left and right, tires smoking and squalling.

In the instant after regaining control of the car, Max slammed on the brakes. A body clad in black tumbled onto the hood and kept rolling down the steep hill. Seconds later, the man came to rest smack in the middle of the street, barely moving.

With no reason left to hurry, Max observed the speed limit as he drove over the man, the driver's side tires squashing his head like a rotten melon.

"Anybody hit?" Leet asked.

Farber answered with crazed blubbering until his faint piping voice proclaimed, "Shai's okay." Seconds ticked by before he added, "I'm okay."

"Good up here," Max said as he drove on at a sane pace.

"Oh thank God," Leet gasped, weary with anxiety. "Get us out of here, Max. Find the 101."

"Sure thing but first we need a new car. They must have hit the radiator." The proof was in the steam rising around the hood, the temperature gauge spiking ever higher into the red zone.

"Ah, fuck me," Leet groaned.

Nice thought but no time, Max almost said.

Pulling his mind from the gutter, he spied a possible escape from their dilemma down the street on the right side, where about a dozen cabs and Ubers sat queued in a line before the porte-cochere of a ritzy hotel. "Perfect," he muttered, pulling the steaming, bullet-riddled SUV to a halt behind the last car in line, a Mitsubishi Outlander sport, a smaller SUV than the towering Xterra. A sticker in a lower corner of the rear window read AWD. *Good.* All wheel drive would be essential if they were forced off road.

"What are you doing?" Leet asked, voice laden with apprehension.

"I'm going to grab my pack, while you put your badge to work and commandeer that car." He pointed through the steam cloud at the Mitsubishi, then opened the door. "You two stick with me."

He didn't wait for affirmations but headed straight for the rear to grab his backpack.

Daniel and Shai joined him, the former looking like a sinner who had just attended an open house in purgatory. *I'm surprised his hair didn't turn white.* Even Max had to silently concede that the encounter had been one of his hairiest to date, at least out in the civilian world. Max caught another glimpse at the ever-present briefcase in Daniel's hand. *Whoever is after this wants it bad.*

Despite her relative cool under fire, Leet was failing miserably in her attempt at grand theft auto. "Bitch, I don't care who you work for, you ain't takin' my car!" the driver protested.

"Exit the vehicle, sir, or I'll arrest you for obstruction—"

Max tuned her out as he opened the rear hatch on the Mitsubishi and stowed his bag. "You guys load up," he said to the Farbers. "I'll handle this."

"Hey!" said the driver, turning around in his seat. "Get your shit outta my car! What the fuck?"

Max closed the hatch. As he came around the car, the fuming driver got out.

"Sir, remain—" Leet caught herself before making the mistake.

Her failure to control the situation surprised Max, her inexperience on full display. He approached the driver, a young man dressed in a baggy white t-shirt and jeans, a white ball cap turned backward on his head. In addition to appearing extremely pissed—and rightly so—he also looked like he could take a punch or three. Max could tell that he was lean and ripped beneath those baggy clothes, maybe even an amateur boxer or MMA student in his spare time. One thing was for certain: Leet and her badge didn't frighten him in the least.

Still high on adrenaline from the gun battle and drive, Max would gladly have gone a few rounds with him just to burn off some excess energy. No time for that. This needed to be handled as quickly as possible.

"Get the fuck out my face, bitch, 'fore I feed you that badge!" he shouted at Leet. He then turned and saw Max coming. "Who are you, her muscle?" He waggled two fingers in a *come on* gesture. "Bring it, muthafucka!" He didn't wait on Max but rather advanced, keeping his eyes locked on Max's like a properly trained fighter.

Definitely not afraid. Max raised the can of pepper spray in his right hand, yet staid his trigger finger when he saw Leet come up behind the driver, who cried out and spasmed when she jabbed a stun gun into his back, staggering him just long enough for Max to smash his nose with a hard left that sent him reeling back toward Leet. She shocked him again and then pressed her advantage, tripping the guy and slamming him hard to the pavement.

Not surprisingly, he started to get up immediately.

Sorry, pal. Max put a big boot in his ribs, then stomped his head into the asphalt, breaking teeth.

And still the guy wasn't done.

Fuck! Max stooped, fired a thick stream of pepper spray directly into his face that left him writhing and howling in agony. He held no malice toward the driver, merely took appropriate action to accomplish his mission. *The Marquess of Queensberry be damned.*

Max turned to Leet and nodded approval. "You're learning. You drive." He rounded the car to ride shotgun.

Leet took off just as bystanders showed up, drawn by the commotion. Flashes on cell phone cameras blinked behind them as they fled the scene. "Dammit!" Max hoped the incident wouldn't wind up on the 11 o'clock news. *Doubt it. They'll be more concerned with the four dead men we left behind.* The thought provided little solace, however. *If only I'd moved faster.*

"So who do you think jumped us?" Max muttered, keeping his voice low for the benefit of Daniel and Shai.

"Not sure, but I think they were Asian. I got a good look at the guy on the dumpster after I dropped him."

"North Koreans? Chinese intelligence, maybe?" Max hadn't noticed the races of the men blocking the alley; it had been too dark.

"One way to find out. The guy on the roof dropped his gun in my lap when you hit the brakes. Take a look; it's in my purse."

Max dipped into her leather handbag, pulled out a silenced 9mm pistol remarkably similar to a Beretta M9. "Chinese for certain, model T75."

"Marvelous, huh?"

"Yeah, perfect." He stuck the gun back in her purse. "So where to?"

"Not back to the safehouse, that's for sure. We'll head south on 101. Bay Bridge is out. No tolls eastbound but still surveillance cameras."

"Gotcha. And then?"

"Haven't gotten that far yet. Maybe back to LA. They might not be expecting us to backtrack after this."

Max tossed her plan the instant she uttered it. *Won't work, they'll still be watching LA. They want to keep us cornered out here.* But driving across the country didn't sound like a viable plan either. *I can't stomach three thousand more miles of this shit. We need to hop a private jet from a really private airport. And I know just the one.*

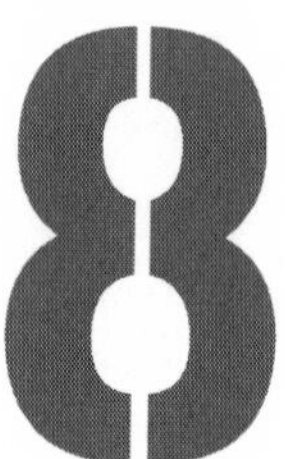

Leet led the way into their accommodations for the remainder of the night, a double room in a seedy motel near the town of Merced in the San Joaquin Valley. As much as Max wanted to keep driving through the night, he had to consider those under his protection, and neither he nor Leet would be worth a damn without a solid plan and some rest. Max could smell the room before he stepped over the threshold: a multi-pronged funk of mold, stale cigarettes, rotten ass, and utter despair. He closed the door behind them, not that it would do much good if they were discovered. The flimsy door might as well have been cardboard, and the cheap locks would easily yield before determined intruders.

Leet sighed after turning on the lights. "Home sweet home. Let's make the best of it." She threw her bag on the nearest bed, instructed Daniel and Shai to take the other at the back of the room near the bathroom door.

"You might want to strip the bedspreads," Max said. "They don't make a habit of washing them."

"Good point," Leet agreed, doing just that. "You don't carry a black light, do you?" She smirked as she spoke.

"No."

"Good thing. Curiosity might have gotten the better of me."

"Some things are best left unknown."

The graying white sheets didn't look much cleaner than the bedspreads, but he assumed they'd been washed since their last use. Not that it really mattered. They would all sleep in their clothes, ready to make a hasty departure if necessary.

Max checked the bathroom while the others settled in. A couple of startled roaches scurried for cover beneath the toilet. The bathroom featured not only a grimy shower stall but also a jacuzzi tub. *Not on your life.* God only knew what microbial filth might be lurking in the piping. As he'd expected, the bathroom had no windows. *Good.* They would only have to monitor the front door and the picture window beside it. Satisfied that no threats would come from this quarter, he returned to the room.

"Ew, that's fucking gross," Leet said, peering behind the nightstand. "Sorry, Shai."

Max leaned over next to her, saw the discarded rubber lying on the carpet. "Not exactly surprising. They rent rooms by the hour for a reason."

"No-Tell Motel," Leet said, shaking her head.

"Yep, hot sheet heaven."

"I need a shower," Daniel said. "Is the bathroom safe?"

"Well, you won't get shot at," Max said. "But you might contract athlete's foot. Maybe something worse if you brave the hot tub. You've been warned."

"Then I shall stick to the shower." Daniel headed into the bathroom and closed the door. As ever, he brought his briefcase with him.

"He never lets that out of his sight, does he?" Max asked.

"Nope," Leet said. "He doesn't even trust me with it."

"Smart man. No offense."

She shrugged, sat down in a chair next to a small round table. "None taken. Who could blame him after being double-crossed so many times?"

"Good point." Max sat down across from her. They needed to talk strategy and forge a plan, among other things.

Shai sat on the far bed, dragging and tapping a stylus on the screen of his tablet and looking thoroughly absorbed. Max craned his neck for a better view of the tablet screen. The kid was playing Tetris, rotating each block the instant it appeared, always thinking several seconds ahead. *Smart kid but a little strange. You'd think he would have been shitting his pants during that attack, not so much his father. Kids are adaptable.* He briefly thought back to some of the kid soldiers he had encountered while in Africa.

"Tell me something," Max said quietly. "Why did Farber flee Israel? A man that brilliant… you'd think his government would want to protect him and use Nexus against their enemies. They certainly have enough of them."

"That's exactly what they wanted, only they weren't interested in protecting him so much as having their scientists commandeer his project. After he refused them, your old pals at the Agency wasted no time trying to get to him. I don't know all the details, but needless to say it was a screw job."

"Shocking."

"And you know what happens to people who won't cooperate with the CIA."

Yeah, they send a guy like me to persuade them. "Did they threaten the boy as well? Is that why he's here? Because if not—"

"Margaret?" said Shai, who seemed to have materialized at the table as though from thin air. He'd discarded his tablet, but the stuffed rabbit remained in his grasp.

Leet put on her warmest smile. "Yes, darling?"

"Can you read me a bedtime story?"

"I certainly can."

"You move like a shadow, Shai," Max said. "You want to be a ninja when you grow up?"

"No." He averted his eyes from Max's "I want to be a scientist like my father."

"Good answer." He ruffled what little remained of his hair.

Leet escorted Shai back to bed and began reading a Peter Rabbit story to him. Max remembered Peter Rabbit and a host of other storybook characters, though not from his own youth. His father had read only newspapers, outdoor magazines, and pulp novels; his mother read nothing at all, unless booze labels counted. But Max remembered reading bedtime stories to David, even if they were few and far between. *I was always gone.* It saddened him to think of all those lost moments. *I missed at least half of his life.* He hoped Shai wouldn't have to endure an absentee father, particularly one who would never return home.

When juxtaposed to keeping the Farbers alive, delivering Nexus seemed a rather paltry priority, especially when Max considered what the US government would use it for—perpetuating the status quo, keeping the game of international espionage forever in play, no chance at a future full of trust or goodwill. *The shit I have to wade through over a couple of names.*

While Peter Rabbit stole lettuce and awkwardly eluded Mr. McGregor, Max got busy on his phone, figuring out the quickest route for next day's journey.

Leet stopped reading long before Peter made it back to his rabbit hole. Shai had fallen asleep. The shower stopped running right about then. Leet stealthily rose from the bed, went to the bathroom door and knocked softly. "Daniel? We're going outside for a few minutes, so you can dress in here." She turned to Max. "I'm gonna burn one while we talk."

"Okay." Max followed her outside, onto the walkway that accessed the second-floor rooms.

Leet's idea of burning one turned out to be sucking on a vape pen as opposed to actually smoking, which was fine by him. Other than the occasional cigar when one was offered, Max never smoked, never wanted to. The very smell of cigarettes turned him off, reminding him of his mother.

"How long since you quit smoking?" he asked.

"About three months. I should give this up too, but I'm not quite ready."

"Eh, one step at a time, as long as you're stepping in the right direction."

"True enough. And we need a right step tomorrow. Today was a fucking disaster start to finish." She looked undeniably weary after driving from San Francisco for several hours over a winding backroad that surmounted the coastal range. *Tomorrow it's my turn behind the wheel.*

"I think we can make that happen. But for starters, we need another destination. They'll still be watching LA, every airport and travel terminal public and private. We need to get off the West Coast."

"You're not thinking of driving to DC, are you?"

"No, we'd never make it, and we'd go batshit crazy in the process. I'm thinking Vegas. I know a couple of tiny private airports where we can discreetly hop a private jet."

"How would you know that?"

"I live in the area." Her lack of knowledge didn't surprise him. Ben might have provided her with his basic information, but he doubted she'd had time to peruse it all.

"Are we gonna stay at your house?"

Max had considered it. "Nah, best not. We need to keep moving and get to the safehouse in Virginia. If word's leaked that I'm with you, they're bound to stakeout my house."

Max resided in a gated community. The tight security had always been enough to keep most unsavory characters outside the gate, but foreign operatives would be willing to risk infiltration and perhaps direct assault with Nexus up for grabs. *The homeowners' association would love that.*

"Okay… that's still a long drive. And won't we have to head south first to pick up the interstate?"

"Yes, we will. It's no slam dunk, but I like our chances." Nothing lay to the east of Merced but Yosemite and the Sierras, with Death Valley to the south of that. They would have to drive south to Barstow to pick up Interstate 15 to Las Vegas, bringing them closer to LA than he cared to be.

Silence reigned for several moments, broken by the roar of a tractor trailer passing by on Route 99. Just when Max thought she might not respond, Leet said, "Okay, let's say your plan works, and we hop a plane east. Once we disappear, they'll be looking for us at the DC airports, large and small."

"True enough. That's why we're flying to North Carolina. Not sure where yet, but I've got a friend there who's always been reliable. I'll consult with him before I make flight arrangements. I'll book us under a phony name and false destination, just to be on the safe side."

Leet chuckled out a cloud of vapor. "So you keep a phony set of papers on you?"

"Comes with the territory. I have enemies of my own to deal with, some of whom might be hunting us on this mission."

Leet pondered the plan, then said, "North Carolina… Then rent a car, I take it?"

"I'll have my friend do that for us under his name as an extra security measure. Even if they find out we flew to North Carolina, it might throw them off long enough for us to drive to DC."

"Well, I have to admit it's not a bad plan, better than mine at any rate." She paused, hit the pen. "Shit, my mind is toast since LA. I never would have thought of—"

"Look, don't sweat it. And don't start second-guessing your every move. Just go with what you know, what you've been trained for, and pick up whatever else you can in the process."

She coughed, swallowed. "I learned more than I bargained for at Union Station."

"I'm only gonna say this once, Margaret—"

She turned away. "Don't. Just fucking don't."

"No, I will. And I hope you listen, because otherwise none of us will get through this alive. There's no room for sugar coating in this business. You lost a partner. I didn't know the man, but he was career Bureau so I can tell you this: he knew the risks. We all do, and we've all lost partners on the job. You can't blame yourself—"

She whirled around and stared him down, the tears in her eyes not running yet. "The guy smuggled two guns into the bathroom right under my nose!"

"He's an operative; that's what they're paid to do. And if he's CIA, he knows how to do it better than anyone."

"But—"

"I'm not done. What might you have done differently? Found an out-of-order sign and hung it on the door? Stop and frisk everyone going into the bathroom?"

"Either one might have worked."

"You don't know that and you're probably wrong. Either of those moves would have only drawn more attention to you. Your partner played it low key, exactly as he should have. But the right moves don't always work." He omitted the part about accepting that fact and moving on. *I've probably said too much already, but so be it.* Max needed her focused on the mission, not Wagner's death. And he meant what he'd said—any inattention on her part would indeed get them all killed and put the secrets of the Nexus project into the wrong hands.

She sobbed once, turned her back on him again. Max waited patiently and hoped she would be done soon. Not because he didn't understand her feelings of guilt and liability—he knew them all too well—but because it would be a tacit admission that his message had gotten through, that she would be ready to face tomorrow with her guilt properly stowed somewhere in a corner of her mind, as he secured his own.

She turned back to Max a couple of minutes later. "I'm... I'm sorry."

Max put his hands on her shoulders, guided her a little closer to deliver his final words on the subject. "Don't be. You're bound to lose friends and lovers on jobs, happens to all of us. But trust me, you're more powerful than you think. I can't do this alone. I need you, and they need you even more, Shai in particular. Keep that in mind and put the rest aside."

She nodded, moved gently against his grip toward the door, the memory of the LA incident still etched on her face. *But she's thinking the right thoughts now. She'll come to her senses by morning. Either that or it's over.*

"I'm gonna head inside now," she said in the empty, detached tone of a soldier who had just witnessed a massacre.

"Get some sleep. You take the bed. I've got the chair."

"Are you sure? You should really—"

"I'm sure. I've got a lot of practice." He would awaken at the slightest sound when sleeping uncomfortably upright in the chair; in bed, he might not wake in time if trouble barged through the door. And if Margaret got too close to him...

Yeah. I've got a lot of practice with that too. Way too much. He thought of his dream on the plane. *Do this right—you don't need another actor in your nightmares.*

Max followed Leet inside and locked up. Before getting any sort of catnap, he had a couple of calls to make.

The sign by the highway read Larrimor Motel. Below that crooked plastic lettering advertised FREE CABLE! HOT TUBS! HOURLY RATES! The sun, already blazing at only 0900, drowned out the red neon letters VACANCY at the bottom of the sign, all Max had seen when they arrived, the only portion of the broken sign lit.

Max chuckled as he traversed the cracked concrete on the second-floor walkway, considering the sign. Larrimor sounded like some pointy-hatted wizard from a B-rate fantasy movie. *He should conjure up some painters and masons to renovate this dump.* On second thought, an arsonist or wrecking ball might make more sense and get him back whatever chump change he had tossed into this dump.

He found it hard to believe the motel even employed maids, until he saw a strapping Hispanic woman with long black hair pull a toilet brush and cleanser off her cart before entering a room a few doors down. *I wonder if she'll look behind the nightstand.*

Though not many crow miles separated San Francisco from Merced, the climates were radically different. The temperature in the San Joaquin Valley had already risen to nearly ninety degrees. To appear less conspicuous, Max had ditched the windbreaker for a sport jacket and button-down shirt worn over his plate carrier. The spare magazines for his pistols were now in a pouch at his belt for quick access.

He rounded a corner and entered the breezeway at the middle of the building, searching for a soda vending machine, which he spied at the far end. This side of the motel fronted a pool filled with two feet of stagnant green water. Leaves and litter floated on the surface, and some drunken soul had tossed a few pool chairs into the soup as well. Past that spread the rear parking lot, where a few battered junkers sat amongst burgeoning weeds sprouting through fissured asphalt, their stolen Mitsubishi the newest vehicle in sight. *I take it back. This isn't fantasy; it's post-apocalypse.* He couldn't wait to put this shithole behind him and get on with his mission plan.

"Well, holy sheep shit," Max muttered, a satisfied smile blooming on his face when he saw diet Mountain Dew in the soda selection. The machine even appeared to be in working order. *Wonders never cease.* He purchased a sixteen-ounce bottle for the highwayman's price of three bucks. The robbery didn't bother him, rather a cost he gladly paid for his drink of choice.

All was not right with the world, far from it, but he couldn't help thinking that things were looking up as he cracked the bottle open and drank. The carbonation hit him in the throat, the brief and familiar burn further improving his mood.

He considered present circumstances as he returned to the room, starting with their stolen car. During the drive over the steep grades in the coastal range, Leet had complained about the Mitsubishi's lack of power, equating the small engine to four mice running on a treadmill. *Weak, but it'll get us where we need to be.* It was also a nondescript vehicle, Joe Average economy transportation, and Max knew the police wouldn't be actively searching for it. *Still,*

I should swap plates with another car before we leave. Shouldn't be hard. Max had seen nothing of the motel's other few guests. *Probably sleeping off their hangovers.*

Rounding the corner from the breezeway back onto the walkway, he again saw the maid at her cart, got a closer look at her this time. *Amazon.* Her appearance put him on alert—six-feet tall with tree-trunk legs that ended in thick, chiseled calves. Gym-sculpted biceps and delts swelled the short sleeves of her pinstriped uniform. Her ass might have been naturally big, but a few thousand squats had expanded it to titanic proportions. Her muscle didn't fit her line of work. Max assumed that illegals held most of the menial jobs in the area, and they weren't the sort of people with the time or money to pursue bodybuilding as a serious endeavor.

She returned to the room, shoving a vacuum cleaner before her. With her out of the way, Max spied another maid cart parked before a room down the walkway. *Shit!* He dropped his soda and took off running even as he considered his next move. The bodybuilder would certainly be in on the ambush. He thought of taking her out immediately, yet did not, opting to sprint past the room where she pretended to work. Leet needed his help *now.* He would just have to watch his back.

The door stood ajar a few inches. An angry male voice spoke in a foreign language, Hebrew again, only it wasn't Daniel. Max barged in, gun in hand, saw Leet and the Farbers backed up to the bathroom door with their arms raised, the briefcase still in Daniel's hand. A bleach-blond maid held a gun on them. She spun and fired her silenced pistol at Max, who ran for the far bed and jumped. He hit the mattress, bounced, and rolled off the other side, gained his feet as the maid's second shot barely missed him, the stray bullet shattering the picture window behind the curtains.

As he'd hoped, his abrupt entrance allowed Leet to swing into action. With no time to draw her weapon, she went for the most obvious target, grabbing the maid by her long blond hair. An instant later she stood dumbfounded, holding a blond wig in her hand, revealing a shaved bald head with black stubble.

The move startled the cross-dressing maid long enough for Max to close the remaining distance. He cracked the man across the face with his pistol, knocking him to the floor.

"Look out!" Leet shouted as she dropped atop the dazed man to disarm him.

Before Max had turned halfway around, a speeding locomotive with a prow of shining black hair crashed into him, drove him back and down. Daniel and Shai barely avoided them as they fell grappling to the floor. The maid came out on top and seized his right wrist in a hold, bending it backward in an attempt to disarm him. Leet and the other operator fought on the floor next to them.

Max noticed Shai fleeing the room, Daniel no doubt ahead of him. *Not good.*

With his Glock pointed in the general direction of the Amazon's face, Max jerked the trigger beneath the excruciating pressure she applied. Though the shot cleanly missed, the explosion of burning powder from the silencer caught some of her face. She cried out, blinded in one eye, and released her hold on Max's wrist. It was the only break he needed.

He bashed her in the head with the pistol's silencer. The heavy blow sent her rolling to the side, freeing his body. They sprang to their feet almost simultaneously. The maid leveled a spinning kick at his head that he narrowly ducked. He put a bullet into her, center mass, which knocked her backward onto the bed, gasping. Her body armor had stopped the round dead.

Behind him Leet's stun gun popped, unleashing half a million volts into her adversary.

Meanwhile, Max's foe attempted to roll off the bed and run for the door. *No way.* With the quickness of a striking cobra, he grabbed her flailing right ankle with his left hand, then brought his forearm down atop her knee and pushed with tremendous force. Her screaming drowned out the muffled crunch of her knee bending in the wrong direction.

"You like martial arts, do you?" Max grunted the words with a hint of callous amusement.

He battered her head once more with the Glock, then put his weight behind a perfect left-handed punch that shattered her lantern jaw like a Ming vase beneath a sledgehammer. Blood flew as a jagged shard of her mandible punched through skin. The blow amazed even Max, who hadn't been expecting to break such a monolithic piece of bone, large and calcified from steroid abuse. He shook his throbbing left hand, the knuckles already starting to bruise. *Well worth it.*

Another pop from the stun gun drew his attention back to Leet, who had her situation under control, the crossdresser writhing on the carpet as she knelt over him. His gun lay out of reach by the bathroom door.

"Hit him again," Max said. "It's time we sent a message."

"My pleasure." She jabbed the stun gun under his dress and shocked him, held it tightly against his balls for a couple of seconds.

"Is that the Vienna Boys Choir I hear?"

"No, more like a Mossad agent, I'd say."

Max shook his head as he regarded the bald man. "Sloppy, very sloppy. I thought you guys were better than this."

The man grinned through a mouthful of blood, then spat some on the carpet. "We will capture the traitor Farber and bring him to trial," he said with a faint Israeli accent.

"Correction, your fellow operatives will *try* to capture Farber. But lucky for you assholes, you two are finished." He turned to Leet. "Find Daniel and Shai and meet me at the car."

"What about these two?"

"They'll be taken care of."

"Just be quick about it." She grabbed her purse and bag and hastily departed.

Max knelt next to the bald man. "So how many more of you are there?"

"Enough. We will seize what we seek and murder those who stand in our way."

Max nodded. "Okay, then. Be sure to tell your friends all about me." He grabbed him by the shoulder and flipped him face down. Then, drawing the Ka-Bar from the sheath at the small of his back, he deftly slashed the back of the bald man's leg just above the knee, severing the hamstring. The slaughterhouse pig squeal that followed left Max's ears ringing, but he finished the job and severed the other hamstring. True to his word, neither operative would be chasing them again.

After returning his weapons to their respective holsters, Max grabbed his pack and headed for the door. On the bed, the muscular maid moaned softly through her shattered jaw. "Use a gun next time, sweetheart. Rhonda Rousey, you ain't." *Good thing.* Had she gone the pistol route, she could have shot him in the head the instant she entered the room.

Max knew why she hadn't. *She had something to prove.* He remembered the type from the CIA: cowboys who valued their vanity over their objectives, always utilizing their strongest skills in a fight as opposed to the method most appropriate for the situation. *The most dangerous kind to work with.* He doubted the bald man with the severed hamstrings would consider partnering with the bodybuilder again, if either ever returned to work.

The Mossad's misfortunes put him in a fine mood once more, until he noticed his spilled bottle of diet Dew lying on the walkway. "There's always a catch."

He found Leet and their charges awaiting him in the downstairs breezeway. "You men all right?"

"Fine," Daniel said, clearly shaken. Max wondered what the drag queen operative had said to him. *Not enough to make him give up that case.*

"How about you, big guy?"

"I lost Bao," Shai said, staring at the floor in dejection.

"Bao?"

"His stuffed rabbit," Leet said. "Don't worry, honey, we'll find you another as soon as we can."

Where other children might have protested and thrown a tantrum, Shai merely nodded in melancholy resignation.

"We have another problem," Leet said. "The maids disabled our car, cut every wire in the engine compartment."

"So much for the four mice. Let's find another ride." *Do it fast. More of them might arrive at any time.*

Max led them out of the breezeway and past the sagging fence surrounding the cement pond. A quick scan of the lot revealed only the same broken-down heaps he'd seen when buying his soda. "Down there," Leet said, already striding toward the far end of the building.

"Nice catch," Max said when he spotted what she had in mind: a snot-green Plymouth Roadrunner trimmed in black. The owner had kept it close to factory original. No hotrod modifications, it was pretty beat up, paint faded by the searing California sun, with portions of the lower body rusted through. Though no expert on classic cars, Max pegged it for late 60s vintage. The number 383 was painted beside the hood vents. *They don't make engines that big anymore.*

"Let's hope it runs better than it looks," Max muttered. The owner likely resided behind the nearest door, passed out in a drug coma if luck was with them. "I'll get us inside." He made for the small window behind the driver's seat, ready to smash it so he could pull the door lock knob.

"No, let me," Leet said, pulling from her purse an object resembling a twelve-inch steel ruler. "Old cars are a cinch."

True to her claim, she slim-jimmed the Road Runner in under ten seconds. They quickly ushered Daniel and Shai into the back seat. Leet got behind the wheel and began hotwiring while Max grabbed shotgun.

Leet's prowess at car theft astounded him; she actually carried a small hotwiring kit in her purse. The 383 roared into fiery life less than a minute later, generating enough racket through dual glasspack mufflers to notify the owner if he was in earshot. She put it in first gear and slowly pulled away, navigating around the Larrimor Motel.

"How the hell did you do that so fast?" Max asked, feeling somewhat jealous. *Not bad for a Fed. I'd still be searching for the right wires.*

"Would you believe I used to repo cars on my summer breaks during college?" She gunned the engine and plowed through the weedy lot toward Route 99.

Max laughed. "I would now."

"One of our customers dealt in classic cars. Damn, I loved those jobs."

"It shows." He switched on the radar detector on the dashboard, anticipating a need for it very soon.

"We even have a full tank of gas."

"Great. I wonder how many yards she gets per gallon."

"Not many. But there are slower ways to get to Vegas. Hang on, kids." Barely slowing to check traffic, she floored the gas and fishtailed onto the vacant highway in a cloud of rubber smoke.

Max pictured Daniel in the back seat, fingernails digging into the armrest as he hung on for dear life. Yet over the hammering engine he heard Shai hollering like a kid on a roller coaster. *Good, he needs that.*

As they hurtled down the road at ninety miles per hour, Max glanced into the side mirror. A white panel van pulled into the motel lot, now nearly a mile behind them. *And that we don't need.* Of course, the van might have belonged to just anybody. *Yeah, and I fly a broom at night.* "Faster. I'll mind the radar detector."

Leet hesitated, glanced over at him, and realized he must have seen something. A bit shaky, she dropped her foot a little further.

Shai laughed and hooted uproariously in the back seat.

10

They sat in a diner at a truck stop about twenty miles from Vegas, each silently relishing the air conditioning and the food just set before them. "Doesn't look bad," Max commented. "I'm hungry enough to eat a steak from a truck stop."

"Eh, mine could look better." Leet sat across the table, next to Shai. "I thought truckers were known for demanding good food." She picked critically at her grilled chicken salad, the lettuce a bit brown and wilted.

"I don't think many truckers go for the grilled chicken salad." Max cut into his steak, pleased to find it rare as he'd requested. "But who knows? Seems everyone is a health nut these days."

"Or so they claim. And how is yours, darling?" she asked Shai, who gave her a thumbs up as he chewed on a cheeseburger.

"We don't eat like this at home." Daniel had opted for a double cheeseburger with bacon and a shitload of other toppings. "I have missed America, despite this ordeal."

"You'll be enjoying it more very soon," Max said. *God willing.*

They'd had it pretty easy since leaving the motel—no one else tried to assassinate them, anyway—yet their trek had been fraught with minor inconveniences, starting with the Road Runner. Its original owner must have lived in a cooler climate or appreciated roasting in his car, for he'd neglected the option of air conditioning, leaving the foursome with only open windows to combat the ninety-five-degree temperature. *At least it's a dry heat, kind of like riding in a convection oven.*

Fortunately, the breeze blasting through the windows had somewhat drowned out the noise on the radio, country music, Daniel and Shai's preferred genre, though it wasn't Max's first choice in music. *Guess it beats what passes for pop music these days.* Their tastes didn't surprise him, however. Many foreigners still envisioned the US as a cowboy culture, having been raised on Clint Eastwood spaghetti westerns. Daniel knew better after spending many years studying in the US, but some men were romantics at heart, Max supposed. *Why can't he dream of being a rock star instead of a cowboy?*

Max had already filled the Road Runner with fuel and octane boost, which the owner had been nice enough to leave under the driver's seat. Now he filled himself in earnest, though he remained diligently on the job, watching cars through the plate glass windows up front and observing patrons as they entered. They might have given all of their numerous pursuers the slip, but he sure as hell wasn't counting on it. Leet faced and observed the rear of the lot, where they'd parked the car out of sight between two disconnected trailers. They sat close to the short hallway leading to the rear exit, just in case.

Max hadn't finished half of his steak when he saw them, three younger men walking across the lot from an SUV. Silver Suburban or Durango, he couldn't tell from this distance. But the men were obvious enough. Decked out in slacks and sport jackets sans ties, they looked like a trio of young professional coworkers on a road trip to Vegas, ready and eager to sample the delights of sin city. At least that was the impression they meant to convey, enough to fool the average person. As they crossed the parking lot, their friendly smiles couldn't mask the tension in their gaits. Even though two sported relatively long hair and the other a cropped beard, to Max's experienced eye, they wore sandwich boards spray painted with big red letters reading GOVERNMENT.

What the screamin' fuck? How the hell do they keep finding us? A microchip tracking device came to mind, perhaps secreted in the liner of Farber's briefcase. It would explain how both Mossad and US agents tracked them. *But the Chinese too? Did they just get lucky?*

He highly doubted it yet hadn't the time to consider it now. "Three agents outside, headed our way," Max muttered to Leet.

"Agency?"

"Or Bureau. How's the car look?"

"Haven't seen anyone."

"Good. Let's move." Max tossed sixty bucks on the table and stood. "Quick, follow me."

The Farbers knew the drill. Daniel gulped, and not on his double cheeseburger, but asked no questions. He dropped his food and grabbed his case from beneath the table.

"We have to go, Shai." Leet rose and took his hand to lead him. Max had noticed him clinging to her for most of the day, perhaps as a replacement for his lost rabbit.

Max took one last glimpse through the front windows. The agents had almost reached the door. He led his group to the rear exit and opened the steel door a crack to peer outside. No one blocked access to the car. *No one you can see.* But he would worry about that when and if he saw them. He drew his pistol, then took off for the car at an easy jog so the Farbers could keep up.

Lacking the key to the Road Runner's trunk, they had been forced to lock the car to secure the luggage in the back seat. Despite

Leet's formidable skills at auto theft, they would lose precious time breaking in and striking the wires to start the vehicle, which they reached in a few seconds.

"Get down," Max said to Farber, motioning for him to take cover behind the car's fender. "Help me out; watch the rear door."

Daniel nodded, his eyes betraying his fright.

Past the Road Runner lay a copse of desiccated desert scrub bordering a drainage ditch at the edge of the lot. Max turned his attention to the brush as Leet got busy popping the door lock. A bush twitched, perhaps disturbed by an animal back in the scrub, but Max took no chances. Firing immediately at the offending shrub, he heard a grunt when he hit someone hunkered down behind it. *Thought so.* He fired again. The shrub sagged as a fallen man keeled over and leaned into it. Max could see only faint portions of the well-camouflaged corpse.

Gunfire then erupted from the bushes, rapid muzzle flashes that sprayed the trunk of the car with bullets. Leet fell atop Shai to shield him. Max likewise dropped to the pavement, hoping to still see the flashes from beneath the car. *A single operative in the bushes.*

Their attacker didn't stop firing, merely aimed lower to take them out where they lay. His rounds flew just over Max's head. One tore his jacket and grazed his back. Leet's pistol started popping, with Max adding his quieter shots to the mix. Their combined efforts stopped the shooter after a couple of seconds, though they couldn't be sure if they'd actually killed him.

Fuck this. Max stood and shattered the passenger side window with his Glock, popped the lock, and then practically tossed Daniel into the back seat. On the driver's side, Leet got the same idea. With no air conditioning in a desert, what did they need windows for?

Leet touched the wires that sparked the Road Runner back to life.

Max instructed, "Take us around front, we'll shoot up their car."

"Right." She punched it.

The car shot from between the trailers as the bearded agent burst through the rear exit and opened fire. The rear passenger-side window shattered, followed by an anguished shout from Daniel.

"Papa!" Shai cried out.

Shit! Max took aim through the broken window and fired as they flew past the agent. None of his rounds struck home, but they succeeded in driving the man into cover behind a dumpster, where they left him to eat dust. When last Max saw him, he appeared to be talking to himself as he alerted his buddies over an earpiece. Max committed his face to memory, certain that they would run into him again.

They fishtailed around the corner of the diner, found the two other operatives standing to the right in partial concealment behind parked cars. Aware that only a couple of shots remained in his .45, Max dropped the pistol to the floor and drew his .380 sidearm from the ankle holster. He brought it up just in time to lay down return fire. Shooting from a moving vehicle was never easy, yet his opening shot, a real doozy, struck an agent beneath the chin before exiting through the top of his brush-cut skull in a geyser of bloody goop.

But he missed his next shot, even though the remaining agent had broken cover to get a better shot at him. In fact, the guy tried to replicate Max's feat, taking careful aim at his head. Had they stolen a modern car with safety glass, he would have died. Instead the bullet struck the windshield and ricocheted off to parts unknown, leaving behind a large spiderweb crack. *Thank God for old Detroit.*

Max's next two shots missed as the man ducked back into cover between the cars. The Road Runner blasted past his position. He fired upon them until Leet wrenched the wheel and rounded to the front of the diner. She nearly struck an elderly couple crossing the lot, who fled screaming before the prow of the speeding Road

Runner, the guy dragging his stumbling wife from its path at the last second.

"That silver SUV." Max pointed. "Shoot the tires. I'll cover us."

People smoking outside the diner scattered, shouting in panic when Leet fired on the SUV. A smart move on their part, but falling flat or finding cover would have served them better, for Max's last nemesis soon appeared at the corner of the building. Expecting his arrival, Max squeezed off two shots, one chipping the brick. The operative leaned out to return fire. Max tagged him high in the shoulder as they exchanged lead. One of the fleeing smokers ran into the line of fire, a cigarette still hanging in his mouth. An enemy bullet passed cleanly through his neck before bouncing off the Road Runner's stout quarter panel. A woman following the victim came to a dead stop at his body, wailing in terror. She would likely die next, though not by Max's hand.

"Go!" he shouted once Leet had taken out the front tires.

They took off, the force of the accelerating car pressing Max into the vinyl bench seat. More screaming followed them, accompanied by the ping of two bullets striking the rear of the car. Out on the road, a line of cars and rigs stood backed up at a red light.

"Hang a right," Max said.

"The interstate's left."

"Just do it. I know where I'm going." Traffic was clear in that direction, the road an older two-lane route that would still get them to Vegas, only not quite as fast.

"Anyone following us?"

Max looked back. The operative had already fled the murder scene, and no vehicles followed. He watched two cars crash head-on in the parking lot, air bags erupting in the faces of their terror-stricken drivers. "No, we're clear for the moment."

In the calm that followed, Max remembered Daniel, wounded in the back seat. He turned to evaluate his condition. The bullet had struck him squarely in the right arm and lodged there. The wound bled profusely. Shai used a t-shirt from his bag as a makeshift bandage as he attempted to stanch the bleeding, his coolness again amazing Max. But for the instant Daniel had been shot, Shai remained remarkably calm and quiet.

"Is it bad?" Leet asked. "Does he need a doctor?"

"I'd say so."

She smacked the steering wheel. "Dammit! And the ER is out of the question."

"Don't worry, I know a doc who doesn't ask any questions. And he makes house calls for the right price."

"You didn't change your mind, did you? We're not going to your house?"

"No."

He checked his watch: 1725. Their flight didn't depart until 2200. He'd been planning to kill the time by waiting in a secluded lot near Mount Charleston, access for a local hiking trail. No one would search there, and it had enough trees to conceal them from eyes in the sky. *So much for that.* But things could have been much worse: Farber mortally wounded, or Max in a strange city where he had no connections. Compromised or not, Vegas had been the right move.

"So where to?"

Max smirked. "Just stay on this road. You're about to see Vegas like a native."

11

"Yello?" a Texan twang drawled into Max's ear.

"Hey, Sharp, it's Max." Sharp owned Sharp's Shooting Gallery, around the corner from the shithole motel on Fremont, east of downtown Vegas, where Max had secreted them for the moment.

"Well no shit, I got caller ID." He laughed. "So what you been—?"

"No time for chitchat. You at the range or the bar?"

"The Wheel, where else? Work is highly overrated." Sharp saddled his assistant manager with most of the responsibility of running the indoor shooting range, while he sat playing video poker at the Golden Wheel, a seedy biker joint across the street.

"Do me a favor. I'm over at the Old Stage Motel—"

He cut Max off with his barking laugh. "What the fuck you doin' there? I didn't know you smoked meth. That's a welfare joint now; you know that, right?"

"Didn't have many options. Look, I need you to stir up some of the locals, get 'em on the lookout for any vehicles that look even remotely government—CIA, FBI, whatever. Any kind of suits. Cops too, uniform or otherwise. God knows they're a rare enough sight down here." Figuring the Agency would keep their quest for Nexus under wraps, Max didn't expect them to involve the cops, but he had to anticipate the worst.

A pause on the line. "Uh-huh... Well, there ain't much love for the gubment 'round here, that's true, but I'll need some incentive."

"Spread the word that there's some kind of sting operation in the works, then buy the bar a couple rounds of drinks to get 'em in the mood and out on the streets. Bill me for it, and I'll flip you a couple grand to boot next time I see you."

"Okay, I guess I can do that. You must be in some serious shit."

"Neck deep, pal. I sure appreciate it. Call me if anyone spots anything."

"Will—"

Max terminated the call, confident that the Wheel's patrons would be on alert the moment they finished their shots. The bar hosted at least half a dozen hardcore felons at any hour of the day, as well as shooting enthusiasts of the minuteman type who distrusted every government agency. In addition to its close proximity to Sharp's, Max chose the Old Stage because law enforcement avoided this ugly portion of Vegas; the neighborhood didn't generate enough tax revenue for the city to care about it. It didn't look like much of a ghetto compared to those in most major cities—not a lot of graffiti or burned-out houses—but the poverty and despair were every bit as palpable.

Max turned his attention back to Leet and the others in the room, which now included Dr. Coddington, the retired Air Force surgeon whom Max sometimes called upon when he needed to avoid the ER. He'd been waiting for them when they arrived, locked in his black BMW with the engine running.

"Ready when you are, Max." Coddington stood beside the blood-stained mattress where Daniel lay ready for surgery.

The doc had administered local anesthetic for the operation, but he didn't think it would totally dull Daniel's pain. The bullet was lodged very deep in his shoulder joint. Max and Leet would have to hold him down during the extraction. Shai looked stunned, detached from reality as he watched his father bleed.

"Gotcha, Doc, just a second." Max checked the door, its locks busted from his break-in. He hadn't known the Old Stage had become a welfare motel, though it actually worked to their advantage: a disgusting but free room with no desk clerk for the Agency to bribe or coerce into snitching.

Peering outside, he saw the Road Runner parked beneath a sagging, rusted carport that ran along an equally saggy chain-link fence bordering the property. On the way into town Max had visited a speed shop and purchased a tarp for the car. The carport shed had collapsed completely in a spot or two, the wreckage helping to further conceal the Road Runner. He saw no suspicious government types around, though two of the motel's residents had ventured outside for evening cocktails, each sipping from a bottle in a paper sack as they sat on rickety lawn chairs outside the room next door.

Max slipped outside and approached them.

"Wassup, high roller?" rasped the first derelict, an old white guy with a braided yellow beard and the withered body of a terminal cancer patient.

"Strip's down there, chief," said his companion, a large black man stuffed into tattered, ill-fitting woodland camo from the local Goodwill. He kindly pointed the way before hitting his bottle of Night Train. "That your car?" He nodded at Coddington's beamer.

"Yep. You guys mind watching it for me while I take care of some business?"

Both bums laughed, the black one waving a dismissive hand. "Man, get the fuck outta here."

"Five hundred each." Max pulled out a roll of cash.

"Huh?" The black guy nearly dropped his wine.

"You heard right." Max proffered the money yet withdrew when the bums greedily reached for it. "There's one more thing I need you to do, real easy. You see any cops cruise the lot, any suits who look undercover, you let me know. Deal?"

"Fuck yeah!" said the white bum as he grabbed the cash.

Max nodded, then donned his most menacing look. "Stay here till I leave. You can go lose it after I'm gone. Don't fuck me over, boys. I don't forget faces."

"Ain't no thang, chief," the black bum said. "We be right here in wine country."

You fucking better be. Max went back inside and closed the busted door behind him as far as it would go.

Hellhole didn't begin to describe the room, a regular fucking Hades. The western-themed Old Stage had been a respectable motel fifty years before, but since then it had declined first into hourly status, hosting hookers and johns, before plummeting to its final disposition as the lowest rung of government housing, a recent development that had nevertheless taken its toll. Max had cleared out Taliban bunkers in Afghanistan that were cleaner. Most everything had been stripped from the room—TV, couch, the second bed. They didn't even have running water; some scavenger had torn out the copper piping in the bathroom to recycle for drug or gambling funds. The air conditioner in the front wall had suffered the same fate.

The stench of urine pervaded the hot, stagnant air and made Max's nostrils tingle with disgust, not quite hiding the stink of putrefaction starting to rise from Daniel's wound. *Fuck, he was only shot an hour ago.* But Max knew it didn't take long for infection to set in under hot and filthy conditions; he'd seen it occur many times on many battlefields. *Good thing the doc wasn't busy, or we'd be fucked.*

"Let's get this done." Max sat down reluctantly on the mattress, next to Daniel. Reeking sweat drenched the scientist, a competing scent for Coddington's array of pungent antiseptics. "You're gonna have to wear these." Max produced a pair of handcuffs from his belt, fitted them just tightly enough around Daniel's wrists, though he didn't appear to notice through the fog of the sedatives Coddington had fed him. Now Daniel couldn't flail his arms, which would make holding him down easier. "I'll take his legs; Margaret, you mind the cuffs."

"Roger that." Weary, Leet sounded half asleep. *Looks it too. We'll all feel better once we leave this dump behind.*

"Ready when you are, Doc."

Coddington got busy, the blue eyes behind his bifocals animated and completely focused on his work. He'd removed many bullets in his career, both for the Air Force and his private clients around Vegas. Max totally trusted him and admired the deftness with which he worked. Daniel didn't move an inch as the doctor probed around in his wound, cleaning as he went, delving ever deeper for the bullet with a pair of forceps.

"It appears that the bullet passed through his upper bicep, struck the humerus, and traveled tangentially up to his deltoid," Coddington said. "Luckily, it doesn't appear that any major blood vessels were severed."

Daniel tried to flop reflexively, grunting in pain when Coddington went a little too deep. Max and Leet kept a firm hold on him.

"Here we go," Coddington said. "He's going to flinch again, harder, and probably scream too. So get ready."

It was an understatement. Though Daniel was not a large man, Max still had his hands full when the doc plunged his forceps deep into the wound. Daniel wailed like a cartoon character who had just stepped in a bear trap. His violent thrashing kept Max busy holding him down. Doc continued to probe the wound, coming up a moment later with a mushroomed slug.

"There's our culprit," Coddington announced, admiring the deformed slug with detached satisfaction.

Shai flinched in Max's peripheral vision. *No kid should have to watch his dad go through a back-alley operation.* Otherwise, the boy remained calm as usual, a stoic demeanor Max respected. *Most boys his age would be hysterical by now. Maybe he is a touch autistic.*

Daniel's yelling trailed off as he passed out from the pain and fell into a deep sleep. He didn't awaken when Coddington started cleaning the depths of the wound. Once everything had been swabbed out to his satisfaction, the doc applied a thick adhesive bandage over the wound, following up with a shot of penicillin. He didn't suture the hole, which would have required additional disinfecting in a more sterile environment. Doc pulled out a small needle attached to some tubing and an IV bag with a dextrose solution from his bag. He started the IV into Daniel's arm and hung the bag on the bed post.

"He'll sleep for at least a couple of hours. Remove the IV once the bag is empty." Coddington wiped off his surgeon's tools with alcohol in preparation for the autoclave. As each met his satisfaction, he stowed them in a thick plastic bag so they wouldn't contaminate the sterile packs in his old-school leather satchel.

"But he's going to be okay, right?" Leet asked, dread in her voice.

"He lost a good deal of blood, and his shoulder will require physical therapy to heal properly, but he'll make it if he takes it easy." His bespectacled eyes fell on Max. "I don't know what you're into this time, but you should leave this man out of it. He needs to rest for at least a few days."

Max nodded. "Understood." *He'll have all the rest he needs when we get to DC. Hope our trip to the airport goes smoothly.*

The doctor chuckled. "Yes, I've heard that from you before. Just remember, you're not the patient this time."

"We'll take good care of him, doctor," Leet said. "Thank you so much."

"All in a day's work." He pulled three prescription bottles from his satchel. He shook the first bottle. "Tranquilizers, take as needed." He handed Max a second bottle of pills. "Antibiotics, ensure he takes them with food, three times daily." The third bottle earned Max a glare. "And three days' worth of oxycontin. I hate to prescribe it, but I think it's warranted in this case." He rummaged again in his bag, then handed Leet an arm sling. "He'll be thirsty when he awakens, so try to find some water. And take those cuffs off."

"I wasn't going to leave him trussed," Max grumbled.

"Good to hear. That should do it, then."

Max handed him a roll of cash as he went to depart. "Is five thousand enough?"

Coddington shrugged. "Sure, but I would have taken three."

"Well, you know I'm a big tipper. And I still owe you one."

"Just remember I was never here and be thankful you didn't catch me on the golf course. I'm going to go home now and take a very long shower."

"I'll show you out."

The black bum watched Max seal Coddington in his car and send him off. "Thought that was your ride, chief."

"I lied. Mine's over there." He pointed to the covered Road Runner. "Where's your buddy?"

"Went to get more wine; you takin' your sweet-ass time and we thirsty. What kinda satanic bullshit you do in there, slaughter a pig?"

Max ignored the question. "See anything out of the ordinary?"

"Nah, ain't seen shit."

He nodded. "Good. I need you guys to stay on watch for a while longer." He peeled off two more hundreds and handed them over. "Sure your friend didn't dip on you?"

"He'll be back."

"I need some water."

The bum shrugged. "They's a fountain in the breezeway, cleaner than the tap. I know the last muthafucka got kicked out that room gaffled all the copper. I coulda used that."

"And I could have used the water. But thanks for the info."

After filling their water bottles and his hydration pack from the fountain, Max returned to find Shai sitting on Leet's lap. They spoke softly, just above a whisper, while Daniel breathed laboriously in his sleep. Max checked the time: 1915.

"We need to leave by 2030." Max had booked their flight from Jean Airport, about thirty miles south of Vegas. The jet company leveled a hefty surcharge on him for flying out of the tiny facility, which catered mostly to single-engine prop planes and ultralights, claiming the runway barely met their minimum length requirement. Since it was the only field near Vegas unlikely to be surveilled by their pursuers, he didn't mind paying extra.

"Okay. How far to the airport?" Leet asked.

"If nothing goes wrong, only half an hour or so."

"And what could possibly go wrong?" She gave an exasperated smile that bordered on hysterical.

"Let's not worry about that now. You two try to get some rest; I'll hold down the fort."

"Thanks! This chair is a regular lazy boy." She shifted her weight in the rusty folding chair, miming the act of getting comfortable.

You can sleep on the bed next to Daniel, I suppose. The blood is almost dry.

Father Time rode a tortoise as the minutes crept by. Leet and Shai managed about an hour of sleep before Max awakened them. Stirring Daniel from his coma of sedatives proved more difficult. They got him up and moving, but he was dizzy and not exactly coherent, though he certainly felt pain, judging from his grunts and groans.

"Should we give him an oxy?" Leet asked as they fitted him with the arm sling.

"Not yet, he's still off in la-la land. Wait till we get on the plane. I'll go get the car."

When Max got outside bum number two had returned. "How we lookin'?"

"Ain't seen shit," the black bum answered. "'Cept for another BMW cruised through a few minutes ago."

"Pimp? One of the local dealers?"

"Prob'ly," said the white bum, who now sipped wine the color of antifreeze from a clear bottle.

Or someone else who didn't know the place is welfare, maybe looking for a room to cheat on his wife. "Thanks, guys, you've been helpful. Anyone asks, you never saw me." He gave them another two hundred dollars of Swift's money. "Don't spend it all in one place."

They'd vacated their lawn chairs by the time Max pulled the Road Runner up before the room. He predicted they would be broke again by morning at the latest. *Or dead, depending on what drugs they buy.*

Getting Daniel into the back seat on the passenger side proved a trial that ate up valuable time, but Max couldn't have him riding on the front bench beside him as he drove. Like everything else on the Road Runner, the lap belts were vintage, with no shoulder harness to keep Daniel from flopping over onto Max.

Leet slipped into the seat behind Max with Daniel's briefcase at her feet. "Shai, you'll have to keep your father sitting up straight and pull him down if I tell you to duck. Got that?"

"Yes," he said, the word barely the tweet of a baby bird.

"Be big on the inside, Shai," Max said over his shoulder. "You can do it."

"Okay." All big, earnest eyes, the kid took his duty seriously.

Max adjusted the rearview mirror. "And I have a surprise for you, Special Agent Leet. You'll find a Saint in my pack with a couple of magazines. I've got two more for you." He unbuttoned his shirt, removed them from the plate carrier, and passed them back.

"Bitchin'." Leet chambered a round.

One last thing… Max turned the tuning knob on the radio, cutting off some drugstore cowboy droning over a lost love, or maybe a spilled beer. "Shut the fuck up," he muttered. A couple of moments later Led Zeppelin ruled the airwaves, working through the mellow opening bars of "What Is and What Should Never Be."

Kind of sums up this mission. Max drove through the lot toward Fremont at a leisurely pace.

12

Headed westbound on Charleston to pick up southbound I-15, Max cruised at the speed limit, squinting through sunglasses into the final rays of brilliant daylight.

"How we lookin' back there?" he asked Leet, who sat swiveled to one side on the rear bench as she watched their back.

"A couple of cars have been following since we turned. Blue Toyota compact, gold BMW."

BMW? Checking the side mirror, he saw the sedan trailing them several car lengths back in the same lane, no cars between them. *I should have asked those bums what color it was.* "Keep an eye on that beamer."

"Really? Looks like a drug dealer. Blacked out windows, chrome wheels."

It may have belonged to anyone, as BMWs were pretty common in Vegas, but the coincidence needled Max. He still had hope the car posed only an innocuous presence. He could easily outrun a government Suburban or Crown Vic in the Road Runner, but a BMW could match their top speed and accelerate faster.

"Just watch it." Max scanned the road ahead.

Leet twisted around in her seat. "On it."

"I'm gonna take a little detour; see if they follow."

He pulled into the left lane and slowed to make the turn onto 8th St. No traffic light at the intersection, but a steady line of oncoming cars held him there. And sure enough, the gold BMW followed, pulling up about fifteen feet from their rear bumper. The driver of the car behind it blew his horn, none too subtly urging the beamer to move forward, closer to the Road Runner, but it didn't happen.

"Can you make out the driver?" Max asked.

"No way, that windshield is tinted way past the legal limit. I hope you've got him in your mirror. I don't want to look back for too long."

"I've got him, just sit tight for now." Max flipped his attention from the mirror to the oncoming traffic, back to the mirror, back to the traffic. The BMW crept no closer. *It's got to be after us. Why else sit so far back?*

A break of about three seconds separated the current wave of oncoming cars from the next, which consisted of only a few vehicles. The driver of the car behind the BMW laid on his horn again.

Max punched the gas and turned hard left, fishtailing through the intersection in a crescendo of blowing horns and shrieking tires. Free of the beamer for the moment, he roared down the quiet residential street, doing sixty as he approached a gentle turn marked 25 mph.

"They just turned to follow," Leet said when he entered the turn.

Max floored the gas coming out of the turn, nearly raked an oncoming car. At the end of the street, he made another hard, tire-burning left, then a quick right, hoping the dogleg move would throw them off.

Shit, which way? The next left ran straight for quite some distance before terminating at an east-west road that crossed Las Vegas Boulevard, the famous Vegas Strip. Continuing straight would bring him to the north end of the Strip proper. *Yeah.*

Another quandary loomed as he shot toward the northern Strip at seventy mph. Right would take them back toward the Charleston and the onramp for I-15; left would put them on the Strip headed straight for the busy hotel and casino district, likely choked with traffic even on a Sunday night. Max generally avoided the Strip with its mobs of gawking tourists. Not being a gambler or a fan of the nightlife, he rarely had reason to go there. But he figured a left turn would serve him better, since they knew his general location, and they might have another chase car waiting for them by the 15 onramp.

Go with the herd.

Ramming the Hurst shifter down into third, he jammed the wheel hard left and crossed northbound traffic, engine pounding. Horns heralded his arrival on the Strip. He entered the sparse traffic of the southbound lanes and charged on.

"We lost them!" Leet announced. "They went straight after you made that dogleg."

Max slowed to just above the limit. "Good, that's a big neighborhood back there, might keep 'em busy for a while." Had he known that neighborhood better he would have tried to lose them in the warren of streets. *Good thing they don't know that* I *don't know.* He smirked at his artful dodging yet wiped it off just as fast. *Don't get complacent; they'll figure it out soon enough.*

He decided to take Sahara Avenue, which would bring them to the next onramp for the interstate. Hopefully the scum in the beamer wouldn't puzzle out his move until he was long gone.

In the meantime he kept his speed down as he cruised past the porn shops, strip clubs, motels, and wedding chapels lining the north Strip. Getting the cops on their ass was the last thing they needed. The bullet-scarred Road Runner attracted enough attention by merely existing.

Their luck expired in less than a mile, when a black Suburban shot onto the road from a parking lot, its presence obscured until the last instant by a large sign for a tattoo parlor. Max barely caught sight of the gleaming grill in his peripheral vision as the huge SUV made straight for the Road Runner, intent on t-boning them into submission.

Max stomped the gas, rocketed forward, and rear-ended the compact car in front of them, sending it spinning toward the sidewalk on squalling tires. He bit his tongue on impact, tasted blood. Their nemesis narrowly missed the rear fender and charged on across the Strip, bouncing over the grass median into the northbound lanes.

With the compact out of his way, Max dropped a gear and charged on, back up to seventy through a maze of cars creeping along at forty. He shot into a gap between a car and a tour bus that quickly narrowed as the bus changed lanes. Sparks flew when he raked the front corner of the bus, making good his escape just before the gap closed, losing his passenger side mirror in the process. He dodged through traffic and then took to a clear section of median strip to pass more cars.

"They're still back there!" Leet said.

"Yeah, I gathered that." He swung back onto pavement, glanced in the remaining side mirror, and saw the Suburban hop the clear sector of median to join southbound traffic once again. Leet had Shai and Daniel lying flat on the bench now. Bits of glass fell away behind them when she shattered the rear window with the Saint, preparing to open up on their pursuers.

That Suburban had something extra under the hood, for it had gained on them by the time they passed the Space Needle at the Stratosphere Hotel. The silent Saint softly chattered as Leet initiated hostilities at a distance of perhaps sixty feet. Max rapidly approached the Sahara Avenue intersection. Dismayed he noted the line of cars queued up in the right lane to make the turn. Several stretch limos sitting in the mix might have carried some entertainer and his entourage.

Max slowed to hang the right, planning to cut around the cars, but other cars ahead of him likewise barred the way. The light turned green. The oncoming traffic opened up, so he banged a left instead of a right and cut across the northbound lanes. A tentative plan took root in his brain.

He made it cleanly through the intersection, pleased to see the Suburban falling behind as its driver slowed to weave and crawl through the lines of angry motorists. Like the Strip, this section of Sahara ran five lanes in both directions. Flying past a couple of cars in sparse traffic, Max hung a right onto Paradise just as the gold BMW plowed into the intersection from the north side in an attempt to ram him, flying right past the Road Runner before slowing. Its driver had made a crucial mistake, the hunter now hunted.

Max barreled toward them, positioning the Road Runner to perform a PIT maneuver.

A Vector submachine gun appeared at the rear window behind the driver. It opened up on them in a flash of pulsing fire that cracked the windshield even further, obscuring his vision. Max ducked behind the dashboard as he swerved, the car fishtailing slightly as he regained control. He thought of drawing his pistol, then realized the folly of driving at these speeds while shooting at the same time. Forced to evade the firepower in the BMW, he revved up and passed some slow-moving vehicles traveling in the center lane. Their pursuers passed the center-lane cars on the right and wound up trailing the Road Runner, once again becoming the predators.

The BMW gained on them, the driver rallying so his gunmen could shoot out the Road Runner's tires.

"They're coming up on the side!" Max shouted.

As the BMW pulled abreast, Leet leaned across Daniel and Shai and sprayed the car with lead. The beamer broke off and dropped back. Leet resumed her position in the rear window, still firing.

"It's fucking bulletproof!" she shouted. "I think I got the guy in the back."

She fired again, a full-auto burst that emptied the magazine. Max saw the bullets spark on the windshield as they ricocheted away. *Not good. And the tires are probably solid rubber. Otherwise, why go bulletproof without going all the way?* The Suburban now trailed the beamer by a few car lengths, quickly gaining ground.

They sped flat out down Paradise, three dead-straight southbound lanes. The Road Runner lived up to its name as Max stomped on the gas pedal. Though he could barely see through the trashed windshield, he quickly brought her up over eighty, wind buffeting his face as he peered out the window to navigate. Leet continued firing bursts at gunmen in the following vehicles, who responded in kind, submachine guns extending and retracting from passenger windows.

"Gotcha motherfucker!" Leet yelled.

Both vehicles still followed, but the beamer no longer spat fire from the shotgun side. The golden car dropped back to let the Suburban lead the chase. Max noticed the big SUV taking evasive maneuvers to avoid her shots and wondered if it was likewise bulletproof. *Knowing the government, probably not.*

"What mag are you on?" Max shouted.

"Third." She fired another burst.

Shit! She would soon exhaust the ammo, reducing their defense to a semi-auto pistol. *That's what they want.* Max gained some ground on the Suburban as he weaved around slow-moving cars.

Leet aimed for the Suburban—and punched through dead center of the windshield. The black behemoth swerved, its driver possibly hit, but straightened out within moments. It had lost valuable ground, nevertheless.

"Tires!" Max roared.

They thundered through a green-lighted intersection. An elevated monorail now ran overhead, its concrete support posts sunk into the median. Aware they would soon reach his turnoff at this speed, Max briefly considered cutting across the Wynn Golf Club, which occupied the block to his right. *No way, not in this car.* He stuck to his original plan. Leet's shots came more sporadically, carefully placed and growing louder as the suppressor began to wear out, yet barely audible over the hammering of the 383.

Both pursuit cars dropped out of effective range as Max approached the intersection for Sands Avenue. Opting to avoid the light, he followed the monorail into the Sands Avenue Station, roaring across the lot at sixty mph. Frightened pedestrians scattered from the Road Runner's path.

"Jesus fucking Christ!" Leet gasped as Max swerved out onto Sands. "He ran down two pedestrians!"

"And you're surprised?" *Still learning.* Little surprised Max any longer, particularly the CIA's penchant for running over those who stood in their way. *Just imagine what they'll do to us.*

Their pursuers ran a couple hundred feet behind as he followed the monorail left onto Koval, then right onto a narrow street running between Harrah's and the Venetian. The monorail cut south; Max continued due west toward the Strip, hoping he could make it through the obstacles ahead. He hadn't traveled these backstreets in years. *God knows what they've built in the meantime.*

He drove beneath a Harrah's sign spanning the street. The road turned right after that, toward the Venetian's porte-cochere and valet parking stand. *Fuck!* Seeing nothing but red taillights in that direction, he continued straight, floored it, and crashed through a chain-link fence into an alley running between a McDonald's and another building. By his calculations the Strip lay dead ahead, right past a grouping of outdoor tables where fast-food lovers feasted on their favorite poison.

Forced to a crawl, Max laid on the horn as he approached the diners. Just past the tables, vehicles passed on the beckoning Strip. Several patrons heeded his honked warning, grabbed their burgers, and hauled ass, shocked to see a shredded muscle car approaching down an alley closed to traffic. *But there's always one.* Two in this case: a fat man in a ten-gallon hat with an equally fat wife, who stood at their table gesticulating in anger, signaling Max to reverse his illegal course.

"Hurry up, goddammit!" said Leet, practically shouting into his ear. "They're right there!" She opened fire.

"Move your ass, Tex!" Max yelled out the window. He dropped his foot and charged the tables.

Big Tex raised two middle fingers, his wife just one.

Fuck it, you've been warned!

Umbrellas tumbled over; plastic tables and benches upended, shattered to bits as he plowed through the dining area. The phony cowpoke dipped out to Max's left, while his wife made a wrong turn and ran directly into the wall on his right, bouncing off the bricks. Max might have grazed her, perhaps running over her foot, but he had no time to think about it, as he held down the horn to part the stream of humanity on the sidewalk.

He peeled out onto the Strip's northbound lanes.

Leet and the Suburban traded fire as the latter vehicle negotiated the crowd without slowing, clearing the way for the BMW. Tex's wife fell beneath the Suburban's grill when it struck her at forty mph. An unknown number of other civilians also fell—run over, shot, or simply diving for cover. Max glimpsed one poor soul getting run over after he'd panicked and fled onto the Strip. No civilian blood soaked his own hands as of yet. As for Leet, he couldn't say. She'd fired a lot of bullets in the last few moments.

The Suburban was back on their ass as they headed into the intersection between the Venetian and the Mirage. Traffic jammed the three northbound lanes. *Fuck it.* Max crossed over into oncoming traffic four lanes wide. Horns blasted, including his own, as cars swerved to evade his insane path.

As Max narrowly dodged an oncoming bus, Leet crowed, "Yes!" as she laid off the trigger.

Over the engine he heard the shriek of the Suburban's tires as it careened wildly and smashed through the steel barrier posts guarding the sidewalk, before crashing head-on into the Siegfried and Roy monument before the Mirage. Whether she had hit a tire or the driver, he couldn't say. The fireball outshone the Strip's neon when the SUV exploded, Max catching the conflagration for a moment in the rearview mirror.

After another near collision with an oncoming vehicle, Max spied pulsing red strobe lights approaching from the north, though the police cars weren't yet visible. Given the thick police presence on the Strip, it surprised him they'd taken so long to join the chase. He hung a hard left onto a street that ran between the Mirage and Treasure Island.

"The beamer?" he asked, swerving to hang a right at the next intersection, deftly avoiding another tour bus.

"Just made the last turn."

"Wonderful." *But I'll fucking shake you yet.*

Another line of cars sat at the next red light. Max wasn't sure what road was ahead, but he knew that a left turn would take him straight to I-15, now very close by. Again he took to the oncoming lanes. He raked a vintage Volkswagen bug and then steered around another car before cutting left, rear tires smoking as they scrabbled for purchase. The Road Runner's swinging rear end clipped the fender of a stretch limo, sent it spinning into the concrete barrier at the roadside. Two vehicles following the limo crashed into it, starting a mini pile-up that would hopefully slow the BMW.

Upon straightening out, Max found himself behind a wall of three cars blocking the four-lane road. The far-right lane remained clear, all the invitation he needed. He punched the gas just as the driver in the adjacent lane swerved over to take the onramp for 15 north. The offending car swerved and Max broadsided him. The car careened off in a spin. In the next instant, the Road Runner likewise spun out of control. A car rammed the left front fender, rattling his teeth and sending a shooting pain up his neck. The Road Runner's horn started blaring, wouldn't stop, as he tried to steer out of the maelstrom.

The Road Runner broadsided the concrete median barrier, a hard slam. Alarmed, Max realized he'd reversed direction, now pointed into the sparse oncoming traffic. Most of the cars headed for 15 had stopped behind the four-car pileup he'd started. Other wrecked vehicles sat randomly scattered about as their drivers tried to shake off their shock and pain. Three police cars, possibly more, had turned off the Strip and were now headed for the pileup. The horn kept blasting, impossible to tune out or shut off.

Leet cursed incoherently in the back seat, as Max stole a quick scan of the airspace above them to see if a police helicopter was on the scene yet. *Only a matter of time.*

The BMW deftly cut through a gap in the wreckage. Still somewhat dazed, Max didn't even know if the Road Runner was still road worthy. He found it so, however, when he jammed it into first gear and cranked the wheel, laying down rubber as he pulled a 180, clipping a stalled vehicle with the prow as he maneuvered.

The BMW trailed by less than thirty yards as Leet opened fire with the Saint's final mag. Bullets thunked into the car body, flew past Max's head, ricocheted forward off the steel dashboard. One round somehow found the radio, which popped as the primitive electronics within burst into flames, filling the cabin with the pungent smells of ozone, burning copper, and singed plastic.

Miraculously, Max hadn't been hit. As for Leet and the others, he couldn't say. She continued to return fire as Max passed a string of cars and then hung a left onto the access ramp for southbound I-15.

"You all right back there?" he asked.

"Got a scratch but I'm okay. Solid tires," Leet groused. "Can't you go any faster?"

"Unfortunately not."

Over the non-stop horn Max barely heard the squealing whenever he laid on the gas. Full out, foot to the floor, the Road Runner managed only seventy mph. White smoke billowed from beneath the hood and streamed over the cracked windshield. Not a lot of smoke but enough to indicate that the Road Runner had had enough for one evening. They would be beamer food in a few seconds if he didn't think of something.

As Max drove in the center lane, a reckless trucker doing ninety or so barreled down on them in the left lane to pass. Max had no time to consider divine intervention, pure luck, or civilian casualties when he swerved into the fast lane, slammed on the brakes, and cut off the rig.

Squealing tires and blaring air horn drowned out all other sounds when the truck driver stomped on his air brakes, jack-knifing the tractor trailer across the highway. An instant later the BMW rolled awkwardly from beneath the still-moving trailer, minus its golden roof. Two headless men now occupied the front seat, blood fountaining from their severed necks as the car swerved and drove itself into the concrete barrier at the edge of the freeway, its airbags saving no one.

Max moved to the slow lane and drove on, dropping down to sixty as he tried to baby the Road Runner through another twenty miles. *We'll never make it. If the engine doesn't die, the cops will run us down.* The view in his mirror brightened as the diminishing BMW caught fire. Fortunately, the tractor trailer blocking the highway would buy him a few minutes to escape the police. *Not much time, especially if they got a good look at this car.*

Daniel's groans interrupted Max's reverie. "How's he look?"

Leet glanced over. "Bad. We have to get him on the plane and see to him."

"Working on it. You okay, Shai?"

"Uh-huh," he said softly, the words nearly drowned out by the unceasing horn.

"Can you shut that thing off?" she asked.

"Don't you think I would if I could?"

She sighed. "Good point. Nice driving by the way. I was sure you'd get us all killed."

"Thanks for the vote of confidence, but we aren't out of this yet. We need a new car; this baby will never make it down to Jean. Don't worry, I have a plan."

"Get to it then. This car is as conspicuous as a parade float. It's only a matter of time until we're spotted."

Max passed a couple of exits, the Road Runner gradually losing speed. He didn't want to stop too close to the Strip; that entire vicinity would be crawling with cops by now. The electrical fire in the radio had died, replaced by the smell of burning rubber from beneath the hood. Max guessed it might be an engine belt shrieking when he dared goose the gas pedal.

He took the exit for Russel Road and made a left into the first gas station he saw. The Road Runner's ceaseless horn attracted the attention of several drivers fueling their vehicles, but there was nothing to be done about it. Max pulled to the edge of the lot, as far from Russel as possible, and shut off the engine. The horn, alas, would keep blasting until the battery died.

"Get Daniel ready to go while I secure a car."

"Don't you mean *steal* a car?"

"Cut the semantics already." Max walked across the lot toward the convenience store, taking stock of cars and drivers as he went. *Take anything, just do it fast.*

He spotted his quarry, a relatively attractive blond, walking into the store from her car, a Dodge Neon with faded blue paint. As she approached, Max pegged her for a stripper either going to work or coming home. She didn't have the looks to be a showgirl, nor was she trashy enough to be a full-time prostitute. He stepped to her car, found it locked, so he took position in a shady area just around the corner of the building and waited for her to return.

"Excuse me," he said, stepping out of the shadows as she opened the driver's door. "I'm kinda lost, can you tell me how to get to the Luxor?" He wore the dorky smile and gawking eyes of a tourist on his first trip to Vegas.

She rolled her eyes, sighed. "Jesus, really?" She glanced at the sky in exasperation.

Max seized her arm in that instant, spun her around, and placed his left hand over her mouth as he choked her out with a sleeper hold. He tried to do it as gently as possible, while simultaneously pulling her back into the shadows. Briefly she struggled, but her fire died soon enough as he flexed his right arm against her carotid artery. Perhaps she was returning home after dancing a long shift. Max took her behind the store and bound her wrists and ankles with zip ties. He took her keys and her cell phone, placing the latter behind the car's front tire as Leet showed up, leading Shai and supporting Daniel as he stumbled along in a state of shock.

"That was quick," Leet said.

Max shrugged. "Eh, she wasn't my type. I take it no one saw anything?"

"Doesn't look like it." She loaded Daniel into the back seat of the small sedan.

As Max backed from the space, he gave the steering wheel a turn for good measure, grinding her cell phone to bits. They were back on I-15 in less than a minute.

Several cops flew past them on the interstate. Perhaps they had a description of the Road Runner from one of the diners at the McDonald's. Max kept to the speed limit. The cops didn't give them a second glance during the half-hour ride down to Jean.

Their jet awaited them in an asphalt lot near several smaller aircraft. Max parked the car as close as possible, though it would still be a hundred-yard walk to the plane.

"Daniel's out of it," Leet said. "You'll have to carry him to the plane."

"Roger that."

Max got his first look at Leet's scratch, a grazing head wound over one ear. Though superficial, it had bled quite a bit. *I'll clean it up on the plane.*

Daniel's hair hadn't turned white, but his skin had assumed the pallor of curdled milk, though from lack of blood or pure terror Max couldn't say. They carefully extracted him from the back seat. Max lifted him in a fireman's carry, taking great care not to grab his injured arm, and toted him to the plane while Leet carried the briefcase and hurried Shai along.

A stunned pilot standing atop the stairway leading to the cabin gave them a look of bewilderment when they reached the steps, followed by a penetrating downward stare of disapproval. "What are you doing? This is a private aircraft."

"And we're your passengers," Max said as he hefted Daniel up the stairs. "Now get in the cockpit and get us out of here."

The pilot checked his old-style analog chronograph watch. "We depart at ten, sir, if indeed you're scheduled on this plane. I have my doubts."

Max reached the top of the stairway and stood before him. "No mistake, this is our plane. Now get outta my way and get us in the air."

"I'm just beginning my pre-flight inspection. We will leave precisely at ten. Now let's see some ID, I don't believe—"

Leet squeezed around Max, shoved her FBI credentials in the pilot's face. "Here's my ID, asshole. Now get this fucking plane in the air, or I'll put your ass in Leavenworth for obstruction." Her bloody head made her look like a refugee from the zombie apocalypse, heightening the effect of her threat.

The pilot's jaw dropped as he stood there dumbstruck.

"Well, get moving!" she barked. "They love guys like you in federal lockup. Old, easy prey…"

Max cracked a smile. *Class dismissed.*

They were airborne in less than five minutes.

13

The pilot glowered at Leet through the open cockpit door as she exited the plane with Daniel's briefcase in her hand. She led Shai down the stairway. Max followed, assisting Daniel, the scientist's left arm draped over his shoulder. He received only a dirty look from the pilot, a welcome change. *I'm not the asshole for once. Imagine that.*

Max took his time getting Daniel down the stairs, dismayed once again by the smell emanating from his gunshot wound. His condition hadn't improved at all. *It's probably worse than when we left.* They'd tried cleaning his wound on the plane, but they couldn't get below the surface without potent painkillers to numb his agony. Even oxy wasn't strong enough.

The plane's hatchway slammed closed before Max had descended even halfway into pre-dawn darkness.

"You need some help, Max?" asked the lone man standing at the foot of the stairs, his redhaired and bespectacled friend Otto Christiansen.

Max had met the electronics expert years before in the Marine

Corps and had last seen him less than a year ago. Other than Max, only Otto and Swift had survived the French Guiana mission, during which Otto's skills proved invaluable.

"Thanks, pal, but there's only room for one."

"Gotcha." Otto introduced himself to Leet, who greeted him with openly distrustful professional courtesy. *Who could blame her after all the shit we've been through?*

"Damn, he looks bad," Otto commented when Max reached the tarmac. "Gunshot?"

"Yeah, we gotta get him up to DC in a hurry. You got the car?"

"Right over there." He pointed to a black Suburban parked under a streetlamp next to the squat control tower that governed the tiny airport in the middle of North Carolina's piedmont country.

"Déjà vu," Max said.

"And not the good kind," said Leet.

Otto shrugged. "Rental place opens at eight if it's no good."

"It's fine," Max said. "We just got chased by one is all. How far to I-95?"

"About thirty miles, but I wouldn't be in too much of a hurry. You should get this man looked at."

"No time, and we can't risk hitting the ER. Every agency in existence is after him."

Otto chuckled as if he expected no less. "No need for the ER. My new girl happens to be a nurse. She doesn't go to work until tonight. I'll give her a call, have her meet us at my place."

"Thanks, but trust me, that's not a good idea," Leet said.

Max shook his head. "Afraid she's right, Otto. We've been chased damn near every minute since Saturday night. I don't want to involve you any more than I already have."

"Judging from the smell of that wound, you don't have a choice.

Wherever he's going, he won't make it in that condition. Let me help you out."

Max figured they were safe for the moment. The Agency would seize the departure logs of every airport in the Vegas area, though it would be a dead end. To throw them off, Max had booked the flight into Teterboro Airport in northern New Jersey. He'd ordered the pilot to change course for North Carolina once they were airborne. Irked by their presence, the pilot complied after a bit of grumbling about FAA regulations. Still, eager to get them off his plane, North Carolina was a shorter flight.

"There's breakfast and a shower in it for you," Otto continued. "No offense but all of you smell like goats and gunpowder."

Max hesitated. "Okay, you sold me. But if suits show up at your door by lunchtime—"

"Then I'll deal with 'em. No more arguments, buddy; let's get goin'. I'll grab the car."

***

An uneventful night, Max appreciated it. Before sunup they hit the road. He piloted the Suburban north up 95 toward DC. Eager for Swift's location, Max called Ben.

"Morning," the man said into his ear. "What's your status?"

"Tired and pissed-off, but we're inbound with your package."

"Awesome, glad to hear it. ETA?"

Yeah, I'll bet you're glad. "About three hours."

"Excellent! I knew I could count on you."

"All things considered, right? You forgot to mention someone."

"Right… the boy. Sorry, but I thought he might give you second thoughts."

"So you sprung him on me by surprise? Not cool, Ben. Not at all. If there's a next time, I expect full disclosure."

"I hated to do it to you. But you got the job done; that's the important thing."

Max went silent for several moments. "Yeah. Anyway, what about Swift? You dig up anything yet?"

"Working on it as we speak, and I'm not the only one. For a retired Agency ox, he's pretty elusive, but we'll track him down. Got a couple of leads already."

"Well maybe you can put a couple more men on it. I didn't destroy half of Las Vegas last night to hear about leads. I want a location, asap."

"No problem, I'll put two more agents on it. We should have something by afternoon."

"Thanks, buddy, appreciate it." He hoped Ben caught the acid in his voice. "You meeting us at the safehouse?"

"No, but the people there are mine, totally trustworthy. Leet knows most of them."

"Good enough. I'll stop by your office after I'm done, see how your boys are getting along."

"That's probably not—"

Tired of Ben's bullshit, Max ended the call.

"Well, that was rather abrupt," Leet said with a laugh.

"Well, Ben's got some explaining to do."

"Don't take it personally, Max. He's a good guy, and you've known him longer than I have. And you also know that surprises are part of the game."

"Yeah, I learned to expect them from my bosses, not from my friends."

"On the job he's nobody's friend. You forget that, and you need to get over it. The more you pressure him the slower he'll move."

The fuck he will. Max let it drop, from conversation anyway. *She's right, but damned if I'm going to forget this. And he'd best have all of his resources focused on finding Swift.*

He tried to put it out of his mind as he continued north through Richmond, encountering heavier traffic the closer they came to DC. Things weren't all that bad. Otto had made a good catch. Thanks to his girlfriend, Daniel looked almost human again, though still quite pale from blood loss. A huge breakfast and showers all around had done much to lift their flagging spirits and help them regain a modicum of focus. Otto even supplied Max with .45 ammo and 5.56 rounds for the Saint.

I hope Otto knows what he stepped into. For all Max knew, he might be shooting it out with agents even now. *Or not. Maybe we finally lost them.* Whatever the case, Otto's involvement only added to his sense of foreboding.

The boy continued to worry him as well. Shai hadn't eaten or drank much since the ordeal started, though he seemed to be holding up okay, definitely putting on a brave face. But his lack of emotion toward the rigors they'd endured troubled Max. Having seen more than a child his age should ever witness, the kid could very well be in shock.

After exiting from I-95, Leet began relaying directions to the safehouse. They entered a rundown neighborhood in northern Virginia, about fifteen minutes from DC, with small unkempt houses, cracked sidewalks, battered vehicles parked on potholed streets.

"That's our street," Leet said. "Hang a right at that corner store."

Max turned onto the dead-end street, pausing a moment as boys playing a game of street basketball slowly parted to let him through.

"Last house on the left," she instructed.

Max turned around in the weedy driveway, then parked before a spacious, dilapidated home much larger than the others on the block, two stories and an attic, painted sky blue with darker shutters. It looked older than the others too, perhaps an original residence to the block, built back when the area was still rural. An ancient black man wearing a misshapen fedora above a bush of white whiskers sat in a rocking chair on the sagging porch reading a newspaper, a blanket covering his lap. A busted toilet, an old mechanic's tool cabinet on wheels, bald tires, a broken bassinet, and other miscellaneous junk littered the porch to either side of him.

Leet cracked a smile. "I see Dawson's on the door."

"Hope he's younger than he looks."

She laughed. "Considerably."

They exited the SUV and headed for the house, Leet holding Shai's hand and carrying the briefcase. Max helped Daniel, who was almost capable of moving on his own.

"We don't need no encyclopedias, lady," said the door guard, Dawson, when they reached the porch. Even up close his disguise might have fooled Max, the only giveaway a vague outline of a sawed-off tactical shotgun secreted beneath the blanket on his lap.

Leet smiled at him. "Do they still sell those door-to-door?"

"They try." He didn't look up from his paper. "A salesman came by yesterday. He's workin' the wrong neighborhood."

Max couldn't think of a right neighborhood in which to sell encyclopedias. *These days, who the hell needs them?*

"Well, sir, I'll take it up with the lady of the house," Leet said.

Dawson shrugged, pretended to read. Max noticed a spy hole cut in his newspaper. "Suit yourself... Margie." He smiled but didn't look up.

Leet opened the door to usher them inside. "You know I hate that nickname."

"'Bout damn time," rasped an older white woman sitting on the living room couch.

The relatively new furniture within belied the house's ghetto appearance from outside. But the wasted-looking woman in the guise of a disheveled drug addict did not. She would fit in perfectly out on the street. The FBI had done a fine job of masking the safehouse as a halfway house. *Brilliant. Suits coming and going won't be noticed.* The neighbors would peg them as lawyers or drug counselors for the home's derelict occupants.

"Don't hate me for having a job, Parkinson," Leet said to her, good-naturedly. "Some of us were getting shot at while you sat here on your ass."

"No thanks, I like my job better."

"There she is," said a cheery young agent who entered the living room from the kitchen beyond. "Thought you'd never make it." He wore a simpler disguise: filthy jeans, black wifebeater, wallet on a heavy chain, and a phony tribal facial tattoo. When he turned slightly, Max saw a pistol butt swelling his wifebeater at the small of his back.

"You should have known better," said Leet. "Where's the boss?"

"Upstairs in the office, forging signatures on our welfare checks," laughed the tattoo-faced agent.

"Don't lose track of these two, or you *will be* on welfare. And you'll sure as hell have to deal with me."

"Rough trip, I take it?" He pointed at Daniel's shoulder.

"You have no idea the shit we've gone through, Williams."

"Sorry about Don," said Parkinson.

Max stood by during the brief commiseration. Then Leet introduced him and Farbers to the agents. A bit of small talk ensued. Max wanted no part of it. Swift awaited him somewhere. Nevertheless, he played off as sociable. They didn't seem too interested in him or what they'd been through, focused solely on their own jobs here and now. *You might have your hands full.* Leet would have to brief them. He needed to go.

"Let me get these two upstairs," Williams said.

"Max, I thank you for all your help," Daniel said, shaking his hand weakly.

"You're a tough man. Most people wouldn't have made it this far, with or without my help." He turned his attention downward to Shai. "That goes for you too, partner. You're more of a man than most men."

When they shook hands, Shai confirming Max's words with an abnormally strong grip. "Thank you, Max. I hope you find who you're looking for."

"I will. Have your father look me up in Vegas when this is all over. We'll do some cowboy stuff, go horseback riding at Red Rock. What do you say?"

"All right!"

"Good man." He slapped Shai on the back as Williams led them upstairs to see the boss, whoever that was.

Max turned and found himself in Leet's embrace. She squeezed him hard, didn't let go, and said into his ear, "You crazy son of a bitch." He detected a sob. "We'd be dead without you."

"I don't think so… Margie."

She pulled back, laughing. "Don't be surprised if I look you up too. I owe you one, maybe a couple." She leaned closer to whisper, "I'll be searching for Carter too. Don't tell Ben."

"Not a problem. And thanks. You did a damn fine job out there."

"I learned a lot."

"Yes, you did. One day you might be running the whole show."

"Ugh, that's the last thing I want." She paused. "You be safe out there."

"You too."

Leet turned and hurried upstairs, not looking back. As he watched her go, Max considered other ways she might reimburse him someday, then dismissed them just as fast. *Let her go. You'd only get her killed somehow.* The mere fact that she'd survived working a mission with him was sufficient consolation, one less actor in his nightmares.

Max departed after bidding curt farewells to Parkinson and Dawson, grateful to be returning the Suburban Otto had rented in pristine condition. The basketball game was over, its youthful participants now throwing a football in a front yard. He reached the end of the block, waited for traffic to clear so he could turn left.

As he sat there, a black Honda compact modified into a ground-hugging lowrider made a left, passing right in front of him. The driver, a young man with a cropped black beard, was visible above the tinted, half-lowered driver's window. He didn't know the driver's identity, and yet he knew him. They'd last met behind a diner south of Las Vegas.

"Shit!" Max muttered as the man passed, bound for the safehouse.

Traffic had cleared, so Max turned left, pulled a screeching 180 in front of the corner store, and swung the Suburban back toward the safehouse.

14

Despite his desire to eliminate the bearded man, obviously one of several moles in the Bureau, Max had to carefully consider how best to do it. Pulling to a screeching halt before the safehouse might well alarm Dawson into firing upon him. *He doesn't know the guy is dirty.* Somehow, Max had to inform Dawson *and* take the guy down. And he had only seconds to formulate a plan.

He approached the end of the block. The bearded agent had parked in the driveway and now strode to the front door. The guy looked cleaner than the agents in the house, assuming more of a gangbanger look—heavy gold chain over his t-shirt, backward Sixers cap, lug-soled boots. No bum yet not likely to raise any local eyebrows. He was packing, of course, the outline of a pistol butt visible beneath his shirt at the small of his back.

Here we go… Max pulled to a gentle halt, blocking the driveway behind the Honda. Dawson looked perplexed at his arrival. Max waved to him, opened the door. Beard man had turned to regard Max as well, the expression on his face flat, betraying nothing.

"You forget somethin'?" Dawson called, not sounding quite so friendly now.

"Don't let him in, Dawson; he's a traitor," Max said while watching the mole. He then drew his pistol and leveled it at him. *No body armor.* All the better.

"What the fuck, asshole?" asked the mole, trying to sound indignant. "I ain't never seen you before in my life."

"Save it, kid." Max advanced a couple of steps, pleased to see Dawson in the corner of his eye point the concealed shotgun at the mole. "We met in Vegas. This time you go down."

"Hands where I can see 'em, Green," Dawson barked at the mole. "Don't even reach for that gun."

Green did not comply. "Yo, Dawson, I don't know who this motherfucker is!"

"Doesn't matter, we're taking you in." He stood, keeping the blanket over the shotgun.

"A'ight, whatever…" Green raised his arms.

Max took a couple more steps. "Be thankful it's prison and not the morgue."

Green spat at him. "Fuck you, King Kong! We'll see about that."

Max went to disarm Green, confident that Dawson had his back.

A barely audible female scream came from the house. Two rapid gunshots followed an instant later.

They're all fucking dirty! Max knew it even before he spied Dawson turning his shotgun on him. He turned and fired; the shot wide but enough to throw off Dawson's aim. Dirt and dust showered Max when buckshot struck the earth near his feet. Max fired again, shattered the tank on the broken toilet as Dawson dove for cover behind it.

Free for the moment from Dawson's fire, Max rounded on Green, expecting to see a pistol pointed at him. Yet he saw only the rippling tail of his t-shirt as Green cut around a hedge and disappeared around the side of the house.

Max turned back to the porch, ever mindful of his exposed position in the center of the front yard. More shots popped from within the house. The shotgun and half of a white-whiskered face appeared from behind the tool cabinet, followed by a roar of powder and pellets that flew past Max's back as he ran toward the side of the house. He was chasing Green but hopefully his path of pursuit might also allow him to flank Dawson's position. He assumed a quick, crouching walk that kept his head beneath the hedge, obscuring Dawson's view. The door guard's next shot trimmed the hedge above his head, forced him flat onto his belly as shrub leaves and splinters from the shattered porch railing fluttered to earth. But unless Dawson broke cover and came to the edge of the porch, Max would remain out of his sights.

He crawled a few feet, trying to puzzle out Dawson's next move as he peered around the hedge, gun pointed after his fleeing nemesis.

Green had disappeared.

Fucker could be anywhere! Most likely circling the house to take him from behind.

Max formed a plan in nanoseconds. Dawson was playing it cautious. *Assault through!* He came to his knees, fired twice through the hedge at the tool cabinet to cover his move. Then he sprang to his feet and kept firing as he took two quick steps that brought him around the porch, flanking the cabinet. Forced to remain in cover, Dawson didn't see him coming and reacted too late. Max kept up his fire, saw Dawson's ass, and shot at it as the dirty agent scrambled for better cover. The bullet took him right between the cheeks, a savage colonoscopy that dropped him to the floorboards with an agonized grunt.

Max grabbed the railing with his left hand, vaulted over and onto the porch. Blood leaked from Dawson's sundered asshole as the agent rolled over. Max put a quick bullet into the back of his head and moved on to the front door, stepping on him in the process. *That's what you get playing it safe.*

Thinking he might find Green awaiting him inside, Max opted for a more dynamic entry, barging through the front door only to find the living room empty. Gunfire in the house had ceased for the moment, though a muffled shout drifted down the stairs. The situation tore at his decisive faculties. Leet needed his help, but Green might surprise him from behind at any time. He considered storming the kitchen, hoping to find Green in hiding, but more gunfire from the upper floors settled the issue.

Taking the risers two and three at a time, Max arrived in the empty second floor hallway, which reeked of gunpowder. Seeing no enemy around, he quickly performed a combat reload of his pistol as he took stock. Several doors beckoned, two standing wide open. But which accessed the stairs to the attic floor and the gun battle? *The open doors.* People didn't tend to close doors behind them when fleeing or entering a gunfight.

The first open door accessed a spartan office featuring little more than a desk and an open laptop computer, the screen dark. Two bullet holes pocked the walls; more bullets had chewed up the wall in the hallway opposite the door. No blood had been shed here, however. Perhaps a good sign, perhaps not.

Max ran to the second door, peered in, and saw a shadowy staircase leading upward. Agents might be hiding behind any of the closed doors, waiting to catch him unaware. Again leaving potential enemies at his back, he darted up the staircase, switched back at a landing, and moved up the second flight in a crouch as another gunshot cracked, shattering wood.

Approaching the attic floor, Max got lower and crept up the last few stairs. The view over the top filled him with foreboding. The staircase had allowed previous occupants to store junk and dusty old furniture in the attic, which was piled from floor to sloping ceilings. *Shit. Plenty of cover.*

"Give it up!" shouted an unfamiliar voice. "We might let you live."

Leet responded from somewhere with another shot that splintered wood and shattered glass.

She's at the far end somewhere. The mole agents wouldn't be looking in his direction. *I hope.* But as his old pal LT had often said, hope usually ran contrary to fact. Did they know he had returned?

He stood and skulked into the cover behind an old wardrobe, the attic's musty smell thick enough to overcome the powder smoke that hung in thick gray layers, illuminated by small round windows at either end of the room. Peering around the wardrobe, he caught a glimpse of a charcoal suit jacket, which disappeared just as fast. *The Boss.* He followed, ducked behind a piece of covered furniture, and peeked around it. Two quick shots sounded, followed by three more from another location. Sounds of falling debris followed.

He spied the boss's rear end ahead, the suit crouching as he took refuge behind a sofa covered in a swatch of grimy canvas. Before Max could aim, he moved on.

Another gunshot, then a wail of pain. "Ah shit!" screamed a female voice somewhere off to Max's left through the labyrinth of battered antiques.

"Parkinson!" the boss shouted.

Even with lots of furniture to conceal his movements, Max abandoned his direct pursuit of the boss, who would be on high alert for danger from any direction. He might even have realized Max was somewhere behind him. From the sound of it, Max's target remained constantly on the move.

Max squeezed his bulk sideways into a narrow passage, boxes behind him and the back side of a monolithic china cabinet to his front. He took note that it could serve as cover or a weapon later.

As he came to the end of the cabinet, he peered around its edge through a narrow gap in the furniture and found the boss kneeling in his sights with his back turned.

The boss quickly turned, firing on him twice through the small gap.

Though Max had advanced with his customary stealth, he had somehow given himself away. He drew his head back as the second bullet tore a piece of wood from the cabinet's edge. Peering from cover again would earn him a bullet in the face.

"He's fucking back!" the boss shouted.

Max crouched slightly, put his shoulder into the heavy cabinet, toppling it over with a tremendous thud. The boss gave an alarmed shout as he dove to evade the falling cabinet. He almost made it. The cabinet's glass doors shattered as it hit the floor with a resounding boom that shook the house, pinning the boss's legs beneath it. Through a cloud of dust, Max watched him try to wriggle from beneath the great weight as he screamed in agony. The falling cabinet might have broken one of his legs; the shattered glass had definitely cut him in many places. He waved his pistol wildly about in Max's direction as he attempted to extricate his legs. Two bullets snapped well over Max's head, striking the sloping ceiling.

Max took careful aim, sending one round into the boss's face. The bullet exited the back of his head, taking a large chunk of skull and a sloppy pile of brains with it.

"Colby?" called an apprehensive voice.

Williams. "Is that who you're working for, or do you just like your cheese mild?" Max taunted, grinning with malice.

Silence ensued, punctuated with a gurgling grunt that Max assumed came from Parkinson.

"I give up, I surrender!" Williams proclaimed.

"Fuck no! That time came and went!" Leet shouted. "You aren't leaving here alive."

Max didn't need to hear that twice. He slid right back down the narrow aisle he'd just traversed. Exiting the cramped space, he advanced and found a path through more of the junk up there. He followed this little trail best he could before coming to a veritable mausoleum of mothballed, neglected furniture. A lot of cover but also a lot of obstructions.

"I'll confess! I'll tell you everything!" Williams shouted.

Max paused to listen closely when he heard the first footsteps. He put his left hand to the floor, could feel the vibrations from two pairs of footsteps. Keeping low and silent, he retraced his steps a few feet toward the wider aisle from which he'd entered.

"No need, you slimy fuckstick. I'm coming for you!" Leet said.

"Better watch it, Williams," Max called, voice betraying his amusement. "She's a real tomcat when she's pissed."

Heavy boots clomped the floor as Williams took off running through the maze toward the staircase. Leet fired twice and then stopped, perhaps to reload. But she remained on the move from the sound of things. Panicked breaths drew closer. Williams grunted, followed by the solid thud of his boots striking the floor after he vaulted over something. Max watched from his dead-end hideaway near the stairs. He had a decent view from here over some of the furniture in case Williams somehow made it into his field of fire, but he quickly realized that the shot would be point blank as he felt and heard Williams coming for him.

Max pictured his outfit from downstairs. *No body armor.* At least not when he'd seen him.

Pounding footsteps ran toward Max's position. Leet unleashed three quick shots, a couple striking the tall bookcase to Max's left. Williams cried out, hit, crashing into the bookcase right in front of Max and looming huge in his reflex sight. Dazed, Williams turned and pointed his pistol at Leet, oblivious to Max, who stood not five feet away.

Leet and Max plugged him over a dozen times, his body dancing to the rapid, offbeat rhythm of their shots like a frog zapped with electrodes. Their storm of lead and fire pinned him to the bookcase for a heartbeat before he crumpled to the floor, his bullet-riddled corpse resembling an Old West outlaw in an undertaker's window.

"Shit!" Leet gasped. "Thank God you came back."

"I'm stepping out of cover now," Max announced. The danger might have passed, but adrenaline continued to run hot. Leet might shoot at anything that moved.

Max spied her about ten feet away through the attic labyrinth. All the enemy were down at the very least, yet the whiteness of her face and the tightness of her mouth betrayed that all was not well.

"Daniel's been hit. I think it's critical this time."

"Shit. You take care of Parkinson?"

"No," came a feeble gasp from someplace.

"You'll be dead soon, you bitch!" Leet sneered as she told Max, "Let her bleed out; we have to get Daniel to a hospital." She had to be a bit more than hysterical to suggest that; hospitals remained out of the question.

"Take me to him." Max hoped his voice exuded calm confidence.

Leet had made what would have been her last stand from behind a dressing table next to the window in the far wall. Shattered glass covered the floor, mingled with Daniel's blood as he lay there gasping, the hole in his chest gurgling with every breath. Max knew at a glance that he was lost. *Sucking chest wound. He's got half an hour tops, barring a miracle.*

Shai knelt beside his father, stroking his hair and providing comfort in his final moments. *He knows too.* Yet he did not cry, despite the look of profound sadness drooping his face. The boy spoke with a quiet calm and presence of mind that betrayed his age. Max had seen unit chaplains less mature and more frazzled in the face of tragedy than this kid.

"You were a great father," said the boy. "You did everything to protect me. Thank you. Don't worry anymore."

Parkinson gagged again, coughed a couple of times.

"Go finish her off," Max said. "I don't want any surprises on the way out. And watch out for the bearded guy from the truck stop; he showed up outside. Ran away before I could drop him. He might be anywhere."

"Understood," Leet said reluctantly. Max got the distinct feeling she wanted Parkinson to suffer more for her treachery. *Amateur mistake.*

Max noticed something when he took a knee beside Shai—or more accurately *didn't* notice something. "What happened to the briefcase, Shai?"

He didn't look up from his father. "The man in the suit took it. Before he tried to kill us."

"In the office?"

"Yes."

Dammit! He must have stashed it under the desk or something. Or maybe Max had just missed it, preoccupied as he'd been with the bullet holes in the walls. He heard flesh give beneath a brutal blow, followed by a gasping plea from Parkinson. "Get it over with, Leet! Get the case from the office, and we'll meet you there."

"If you insist," she growled. A single shot rang out a moment later, followed by footsteps as she hurried to the stairs, her mind hopefully back on business.

Max knew the fight had seriously fucked with her head, thrown her professional bearing dangerously off. *Betrayal does that. Even if you expect it, you never get used to it.*

"I need to carry your father, Shai." Max went to pick Farber up, stopped when he heard the front door slam through the shot-out window. He stood and looked out.

Green was sprinting across the lawn for his Honda, Daniel's

briefcase in his left hand. "Fuck no!" Max shouted, drawing his pistol. Green stopped running at the shout but then took off as if fleeing a hungry tiger when he saw Max in the window. He ran in a zig-zag pattern to avoid Max's shots and make good his getaway.

Max had expended most of his magazine during the battle, and he hadn't had a chance to reload. His first shot missed, tearing up turf at Green's feet, startling him. *Shifty little fuck!* He squeezed an instant too soon on his next try; the bullet struck the Honda's roof and ricocheted as Green opened the door to toss the case in. The weasel dropped into the driver's seat and started the car, slammed it into reverse, and backed onto the lawn to circumvent the Suburban blocking the driveway.

Max tried to disable the vehicle with his next shot—perhaps his last. He hit the rear tire, which blew with a firecracker pop. The Glock's slide locked back, and Green drove off as Max reloaded. Spirals of sparks shot from the rim of the blown tire as he departed. He wouldn't get far, but then he really didn't have to. All he needed was a couple blocks' worth of breathing room, and then he'd be in the wind.

And just like that... Max wanted to punch something as failure began feasting on his conscience like a starving scarab.

Leet ran onto the lawn in Green's wake. She threw up her arms in frustration as he drove from sight.

"He got it," Max called to her, shaking his head.

Leet stared up at him for a moment, then directed her dumbstruck look downward to the tire tracks on the front lawn.

"Snap out of it!" Max barked. "Get up here. We have a man to save." *Fat chance but we can try.* To his dismay, Max noticed residents beginning to gather on their lawns, the last thing he needed.

Leet must have noticed, for she picked up her head and ran to the front door. She arrived on the scene with a first-aid kit from the kitchen. Apparently belonging to the dirty agents, it contained the proper dressings for a chest wound.

"Put it on in the car; we need to go," Max said.

"Understood." She seemed to have grounded herself, ready to pick up the pieces in the wake of the fiasco.

As quickly as they'd appeared, most of the gawkers had fled by the time Max loaded Daniel into the back seat of the Suburban and took off. Someone would call the cops. Eventually. *In a suburb we'd be in handcuffs already.* But most poor people chose not to deal with the police unless absolutely necessary, knowing damn well that they didn't fall under the blanket of serve and protect. Max wasn't about to complain as he took off, wondering what their next move should be, what to do with Daniel, and how they might even begin to atone for losing Nexus.

15

A tempest of dilemma and doubt whirled about in Max's brain as he drove, scattering his thoughts into incoherent mental debris. *What the fuck do we do now?*

The bandage Leet applied had stopped Daniel's chest wound from bleeding externally, yet he continued to bleed internally, blood leaking from his mouth in fits and starts. *We can't do anything further. He might survive if we get him to a surgeon in time, but it's a crapshoot.* Max had seen men die of lesser wounds than Daniel's.

Technically speaking, like it or not, their objective was to secure the Nexus project, not rescue the man who created it. It had been drilled into Max's brain during his days as a Marine officer that mission accomplishment always came first, troop welfare second. All fine and dandy when leading a platoon of combat-ready men who knew and accepted the risks inherent in their profession but a lot less clear when it came to civilians in tow. It seemed barbaric to search for a briefcase with a man dying in the back seat.

But where do we take him?

"The closest ER is about six miles away," Leet said from the backseat as she consulted her phone, her fingers tacky with blood.

"We can't go there," Max responded. "That's the first place they'll look for us."

Leet unleashed one hysterical cackle. "Will they? They got what they wanted. I'd say they're through with us now."

"Don't kid yourself. We've seen too much. They won't let us walk away from this."

"Well, we can't just let him die! I know another safehouse in Maryland; we'll take him there and call Ben, have him send a doctor over."

Max snorted with incredulous mirth. "No way. I've seen enough FBI *safehouses* for now. The only agent we can trust is you."

"What about Ben?"

"The guy whose people are all crooks, present company excepted? I'm not so sure about Ben anymore. We solve this ourselves."

"Then fucking solve it already!"

Good point. It always fell on Max to solve the unsolvable.

DC wasn't his town, however. He knew no back-alley doctors here nor places where they might hole up, other than in his storage unit. His few remaining contacts from the Agency were either out of the country or out of the game.

Marklin. He'll be able to help us. Max opened the contacts folder on his phone, bringing up Marklin's name. His thumb hovered over the screen, awaiting the command to press the call prompt. *No.* Max returned to the home screen and slid the phone into his pocket. He couldn't go to Marklin on this one. Chances were good that the general wouldn't want to get involved. Even if he did, DC was a small town in many respects, and no matter whom Marklin called in for assistance, they may have ties that lead back to the rogue agents.

Max knew he could probably cajole Marklin into action, but

the cost would be great with the stakes so high. *I'll only wind up owing him again.* That was unacceptable. He'd done enough weird, scary shit for one lifetime. If he was ever to find Swift and the other killers, Max needed Marklin to owe *him* favors, not the other way around.

"Give me the directions for the ER," Max said.

He didn't inform her that he planned to leave Daniel on the hospital's doorstep like a common junkie. She would have protested and rightly so. The decision sickened him, but he could think of no other option. To make matters worse, they would have to take Shai along with them to ensure his safety, separate him from his father when the two should be together. *There's no other way.*

"Thanks for seeing things my way. Make the next left."

Max dropped his foot a bit yet kept his speed reasonably sane as he navigated the stop-and-go traffic. They traveled a couple of miles, the Suburban silent but for Shai whispering to his father in Hebrew, likely praying for his survival. Max had heard the Kaddish a couple times, and that wasn't what Shai was reciting. Shai might well have thought his father still had a chance, and that destroyed Max. He couldn't have felt any more rotten. How would he explain to a child that they had to abandon his wounded father?

A faint, rattling utterance came from the back seat.

"Try not to speak, Daniel," Leet said. "We'll be at the hospital soon."

"No," Max heard Daniel say, though his next words came softly, unintelligible.

"Pull over," Leet said. "That industrial park right there."

Max didn't question her. Daniel's time was at hand; Leet wouldn't have ordered the stop otherwise. Max turned into the park, drove past warehouses and businesses until he reached the rear of the complex, where he parked beneath an overhanging tree in a corner of the lot, far from other vehicles. He shut off the Suburban and turned around to better hear Daniel's final words.

Blood flowed freely from Daniel's mouth, dribbled down his chin, soaking into his shirt. His stained lips moved. "The case… holds nothing important." His words bubbled forth in a halting, tubercular rattle.

After a moment of stunned silence, Leet turned to him, baffled. "But how can that be? Where is the Nexus project, all of your research?"

"It is with us. I will die, but Nexus will survive, God willing."

"It's with us?" Max asked, not sure he'd heard right. "How is that?"

Daniel smiled through the blood, a crimson rictus, and gazed over at his son. "Shai… is Nexus."

Max sat dumbfounded for several moments as he tried to process this revelation. He glanced at Leet, whose shocked expression bordered on angry. She'd gone through hell to protect a case that had never really mattered. She had read Peter Rabbit to a science experiment.

But Max grasped Daniel's statement soon enough. "Shai is… an android?"

He hated to use the word, appropriate though it was. It reminded him that he was a man in a crazy world full of crazy things he couldn't unsee. He couldn't think of Shai as anything other than a boy. But his unshakeable demeanor, even at present as he watched his "father" die, left Max without a doubt.

"Yes," Daniel said. "The case, just a ruse. I filled it with… Monopoly money." He grinned again. "Shai's body is synthetic, his skin a material of my design. I implanted his… intelligence. But he learns!" Daniel coughed violently for several seconds, droplets of blood spattering Shai, who did not flinch away. "He learns like a boy… only he absorbs *everything*. He has what one might call rudimentary emotions…" He gazed up into Shai's eyes. "He is my masterpiece but more so, he is my son."

Shai squeezed his hand. "Yes, Papa. Always. I won't let your dream die."

"Shai…" His voice trailed off; he remained silent for several seconds. Max would have thought him dead had he not heard him breathing. "I am so sorry. Had I known… your creation would have wrought such *violence*… would have hidden you."

"Have no regrets, Papa. You have always done right, by myself and the world."

Daniel smiled. "I wish it were so simple… and true. And now I cannot atone." Again he fell silent as moments passed, his eyes now closed. "You stay with Margaret… and Max. They will see you to safety."

"We will," Leet vowed.

"Absolutely," said Max, who now completely understood why the government had taken such extreme measures to acquire Nexus—the artificial intelligence it represented could permanently tip the balance of power in their favor. *And they'll know soon enough that Shai is Nexus.* "I won't allow anyone to harm your son."

"I could not receive any truer… assurance." Daniel broke down into another coughing fit, gasped for breath. "I love you, Shai." He raised his arms to embrace his boy one final time.

"Papa!" Shai lay upon his father, breathing heavily, crying without shedding any tears.

Daniel smiled, at peace now. His blood-choked breaths ceased a few moments later. Max had witnessed the final moments of many dying men, had listened to their last words. Though he barely knew Daniel Farber, the man's death—and the graceful way Daniel accepted his fate—hit him like few others had. Max's life often made him forget there were men like Daniel Farber.

Max caught Leet's eye, motioned for them to step outside. She nodded. Shai needed to be alone with his father for a while.

"I don't know what the hell to say." Tears came to Leet's eyes as she stared at the asphalt. "How could I have been so blind not to pick up on it?"

"Don't beat yourself up; you weren't the only one fooled. But we have the facts now. We need to get Shai to safety, see this through to the end. If anyone tries to harm him, they'd better make sure I'm good and dead first."

Leet sighed heavily, looked up, and stared at the sky as she wiped her tears away. Smears of blood streaked her face like war paint. "I'm with you. Let's finish this."

"Good enough. I'll call Ben, set up a meeting with him. I won't be dealing with any more of his *people.*"

"Amen to that."

Max took out his phone and wondered if even Ben could be trusted.

"How's it going, Max? Did you make the drop? I haven't heard from my people yet."

"Change in plans. I'll be delivering Nexus directly to you."

"Why? What the hell—?"

Max digested not only his words, but how he said them—inflection, pauses, any clue in his speech that might reveal him to be dissembling. It troubled him to think that Ben might be part of the conspiracy to steal Nexus, yet he couldn't rule it out after the safehouse. But Ben sounded genuinely perplexed at Max's plan. *Fuck, I hope so.* To think that a man of Ben's character would sell out seemed inconceivable. *So do a lot of other ugly truths.*

Max cut Ben off. "We'll meet at nineteen hundred. I'll call you one hour prior with the address."

"Can't you just give it to me now?"

Fuck no. "No, I'm not sure where it'll be yet." In truth he knew exactly where they would meet, the place he'd used to question and torture prisoners connected with his family's murder. But he couldn't give Ben the address, couldn't risk one of his agents finding out and beating them to the location. He'd walked into nothing but ambushes since Saturday night.

After a pause Ben said, "Very well. I'll be waiting for your call."

Max thought he sounded a bit deflated. Again, he didn't know what to make of it. *You'll know later if he's part of the conspiracy. Hear him out tonight.* "Okay, then. See you tonight." Max terminated the call, then realized he hadn't inquired about the search for Swift. With Shai's life—or circuitry, he supposed—at stake, Swift didn't seem so important at the moment.

"So we're all set?" Leet asked, sounding almost hopeful again.

"Looks like it."

"Where to now? What are we going to do with Daniel?"

"Good question." And one Max had yet to ponder. Usually the bodies he collected during his quest wound up in unmarked graves or carrion snacks, but those were enemies. Daniel Farber deserved better than a shallow hole in the woods. "Does he have any family?"

"Not that I know of. His parents were killed by a terrorist bomb while riding a bus in Tel Aviv when he was just a boy. His grandparents raised him after that, but they passed a few years ago. He never mentioned anyone else."

"We'll take him to my storage unit; I have a tarp and some duct tape there. It'll have to do until we can bury him properly."

16

At 1836, Max backed the Suburban into a narrow alley between two crumbling brick buildings sheathed in graffiti. Countless tv shows and movies depicted the pall thrown over the land in the wake of an apocalypse, making viewers shudder at this dark future for America. Few of them realized that it was already a reality in many areas. For a moment, Max wondered when the world ended in this part of town. Dusk was still an hour off, yet they had seen only a handful of winos, addicts, and thuggish gangbangers on the streets of this blighted sector of old DC, once an industrial mecca.

Max squeezed the SUV past a rusted-out dumpster and maneuvered behind it, hopefully hiding the vehicle from street view. Gunshots and screams attracted no attention in this neighborhood. In return for that level of privacy, he had to accept certain liabilities, such as his car being stolen. Usually he parked near the warehouse to keep a closer eye out; today, however, he wanted to conceal it in case his concerns about Ben proved true. Max had to keep reminding himself to let Ben talk, to give him benefit of the doubt as any brother would.

"Think we'll be interrupted by any crackheads?" Leet asked as she alighted from the back seat.

"It's been known to happen." Max exited the vehicle, his heel crunching down on a heroin syringe. "They leave if you toss them a few bucks. And they sure as hell don't ask questions."

"How reassuring." Leet took Shai's hand.

The boy descended to the trash-littered cobblestones. He'd stopped sobbing by the time they reached the storage unit. There he had impassively watched Max and Leet wrap Daniel's body in a plastic tarp. Still, despite possessing only rudimentary emotions—a concept Max still couldn't grasp—he seemed somewhat dazed and now followed them as if on autopilot.

"How are you on ammo?" While at the storage unit stowing Daniel's corpse, Max had topped off the magazines for his Glock 21. Now he realized he'd forgotten to inquire about Leet's ammo supply. *Dammit…* He could have kicked himself, for he stocked .40 S&W rounds for use in his UMP40 back home. *I could have offered her that too, not that she would have taken it.*

"I'm okay, two full mags plus my sidearm."

"You want to take my ankle piece as well? Clip it to your belt?"

"Shit, this again?" She shook her head. "Why would I need a third pistol? I think you need to tone down the cloak-and-dagger bullshit. You're going to meet a guy you've known for twenty years, so I don't get the apprehension."

"Even after the safehouse? C'mon, you don't believe in those kinds of coincidences."

"That doesn't mean he knew!" Her raised voice echoed off brick. She went on in a quieter tone, "You're being really paranoid about this. Get your bearing on and be professional."

"Fine, let's go," Max conceded, tired of arguing.

Perhaps she's right, but I'll be paranoid until I'm certain. No one liked to live not trusting anyone, but the times Max didn't trust his gut instincts, he regretted it.

Max pulled the Saint from between the front seat and the center console, grabbed the three remaining mags, and slipped them into his plate carrier. He locked the Suburban and led them into the warren of alleys separating the various buildings. He'd scouted the area thoroughly last year before choosing it as his secluded spot for torturing prisoners, even going so far as to map the alleys in case he ever needed to escape. Not likely, as homicide detectives were the only cops who visited this area and only as a perfunctory duty in the aftermath of murder. But Max always chose to cover his ass when given the option.

No vagrants slept in the back alleys tonight; no thugs lurked in the shadows. The only living things they saw were roosting pigeons and about a dozen well-fed rats gnawing on a dog carcass. The rodents didn't even scatter as they passed.

"You picked a hell of a spot," Leet said.

"I'd find a cozy place in the suburbs if the cops weren't so nosy."

They reached the warehouse after walking several hundred feet through the labyrinth of alleys. This side of the loading dock consisted of several archways cut into the side of the building that were once used for loading railway boxcars. Double doors of rotten wood still barred access through a couple of the archways; the others had all been sundered in some fashion, either decomposed or torn down by vandals. Practically all of the glass was shattered in the banks of windows high in the walls of the two-story structure. Ben would likely enter the warehouse from the other side, where there was space to park in front of the truck loading dock.

Max led them up a short flight of rusty metal stairs. An open steel door hanging askew on one hinge granted them entrance. They cut across the long room accessing the old railcar docks, the cracked cement floor strewn with garbage, wine bottles, and bum bedding, yet no bums.

"You should put that thing away," Leet whispered, regarding the Saint. "What's Ben gonna think when he sees you with that?"

"Not much if I have to put a hole in his head."

Stepping into a wide archway that accessed the warehouse proper, Max took quick stock of the place. Shadows, harbingers of another desolate night, crowded in amongst the miscellaneous junk abandoned in the cavernous room: busted office furniture, metal shelving both upright and fallen, a line of very rusty 55-gallon drums stacked two high, forklift skids scattered about or stacked in leaning piles. An ancient forklift sat forlorn a few feet away, stripped of its engine long ago. The walls of the main warehouse room soared upward thirty feet to the metal roof trusses overhead. To Max's right, the building became a two-floor affair, with a flight of metal stairs and a conveyor belt ascending to a catwalk that fronted more storage space packed with detritus of the dead industrial age.

Max always questioned his prisoners deep in the dark recess beneath the second-floor overhang. The place hadn't changed a bit. Small fires lit by the homeless had spread in certain areas, yet none had sparked the building into oblivion.

Leet sighed behind him. "This place smells like pigeon shit."

"I wonder why? Keep your eyes open."

"We're fifteen minutes early. I'm sure we'll know when Ben arrives, provided he didn't get carjacked on the way."

"He's a big boy. Don't worry about it." Max stepped into the room, Leet and Shai close behind.

A faint, lone *smack* marked when a blob of pigeon shit fell from the rafters and splattered nearby. Taking a quick glance backward, Max noticed Shai staring intently at the second-floor catwalk.

"Well, I guess there's nothing to do now but wait—"

"Look out!" Shai shouted.

Max couldn't believe Shai had the strength to shove him so forcefully. Apparently, Daniel had overbuilt his body as well as his mind. *Good thing.* Swift wouldn't have missed otherwise. The boy's keen senses and herculean strength had saved Max's life.

As Max instinctively darted for cover behind the abandoned forklift, something like a speeding locomotive struck him in the small of his back and knocked him forward onto his hands and knees next to the forklift. The firecracker pops of a submachine gun echoed throughout the warehouse, startling the pigeons overhead into a mass exodus through the broken windows. Bullets ricocheted off brick, cement, even the solid steel mass of the forklift.

Shai landed next to him. "He's up there!" He jerked his head toward the catwalk.

"Catwalk!" shouted Leet, who had retreated back through the archway to the loading dock.

"Hola, Max!" a basso voice boomed.

Swift! How the fuck?

"You ain't the only one workin' on your stealth," Swift continued. "But how hard is it to surprise you? You're gettin' predictable in your old age, Ahlgren. Didn't take much snoopin' and poopin' to find your little hidey hole."

"Hope you like it, Carter. I'm gonna bury you here."

Swift rumbled a laugh. "Wishful thinkin', amigo. But by all means, come on up and try." He fired a single shot that clanked off the forklift.

"Did you see where he is?" Max whispered to Shai.

"Just the flash. Between a couple of crates near the middle."

"Gotcha." Max put a hand on the boy's shoulder. "Stay right here."

Leet squeezed off two shots from the archway. "Go, Max, I'll cover."

"Good to know, sweetie," Swift said. "Now stick your little split tail out again." Swift fired another short burst, this time at the archway.

Max tensed, broke cover, scrambled to a rusty 55-gallon drum the derelicts used as a fire barrel. Bullets marked his path, snapping over his head in a July 4th crescendo of sparks. Leet answered Swift with several shots that drove him back into cover. Max peered around the barrel, caught a glimpse of moving black, and fired a burst with the Saint that elicited an angry oath from Swift. Whether Max had struck him didn't really matter; if Swift could still curse, he was still a threat.

Max sprinted for the beckoning steel stairway twenty feet away, firing on the run. Leet still had his back. Between them, they tore up the rotting crates stacked along the catwalk. But Swift didn't remain rooted in one spot and returned fire as he picked his way through cover.

As he ran, Max spied the flash from Swift's Uzi—his reliable, vintage weapon of choice—and put two shots into the vicinity. He reached the stairs and took them two at a time, the rusty metal structure bouncing and creaking beneath his weight. *Fucking idiot, trying to take us out by himself.* Leet fired again. No reply from Swift, who had likely retreated to the second floor, where Max remembered a wreckage of metal shelving, wooden crates, and assorted garbage.

"Margaret, watch out!" Shai cried.

Another rapid burst of gunfire erupted, the high-caliber reports louder than the Uzi. *A fucking machine gun!* Not from the catwalk but rather from behind Max. A hearty laugh heralded more machine gun fire.

Leet shouted something as she returned fire.

Whatever was happening downstairs, Max couldn't worry about it. He and Leet were each on their own, come whatever may. Reaching the second floor, Max immediately dove into cover behind a crate and began hunting for Swift.

* * *

The unexpected arrival of the second gunman startled Leet.

Shai watched with grave concern from where he crouched beside the forklift. He needed better cover now that bullets were flying from two directions. "Get under the lift!" she shouted, running to find cover of her own.

She didn't have the benefit of someone covering her as she raced to engage her adversary with murder on her mind. *Him!* She'd only glimpsed him as of yet, but she knew.

The image of Don bleeding out filled her mind, how his blood pooled an inch deep as it covered the dingy train station tiles.

Bullets chased her into hiding behind a leaning tower of forklift skids. Splinters flew as more rounds tore into rotting wood and toppled the skids, which crashed down in a cloud of dust, but she'd already moved on to take cover behind an overturned desk. Her adversary ceased fire. He might have lost track of her or paused to reload.

She reloaded as well, though she reckoned a couple of rounds remained in the magazine. Charging such awesome firepower without a full mag would amount to suicide. She suddenly regretted her refusal of Max's offered sidearm. She might very well die this evening, perhaps in the next minute or two.

Not before I kill you, motherfucker!

Swift's voice droned down from the second floor—shit talking from the sound of it—but she heard nothing from Max.

"Give up the boy, Special Agent Leet," said her opponent, smug with confidence. She had no idea where he might be hiding now. "The chase is over. We won't settle for Monopoly money. We're going to get what we paid for. Maybe we'll send you a few megs of RAM when we're done taking that kid apart."

She wanted to shout at him, curse him and the bitch who'd brought him into the world. *Let him fuck up.* That thought seemed the epitome of wishful thinking. She shook her head, got control of herself. *Can't stay here!* The graphite top on the metal desk might have protected her from 9mm rounds but certainly wouldn't stop whatever this guy was putting downrange.

Thankfully, he seemed to be just as wary as she was, holding his fire and sticking deep in cover, reluctant to reveal his position by firing another burst. If he decided to open up on the desk…

Lying on her side, she peeked around the edge of the desk through her pistol's reflex sight. Darkness had nearly descended, a blessing and a curse. She saw very little—a broken computer monitor on the floor, two low stacks of skids, the row of rusty drums off to the left stacked two high.

A shadow twitched ever so slightly behind the skid stack nearest the drums. She opened fire, four rapid shots that drove him scuttling for better cover. Bent in a crouch, he made for the 55-gallon drums.

She led him but he was quick. Four more shots and he cried out when her final shot tagged him in the ribs as he dove behind the drums. Presuming he wore body armor, he wouldn't be in pain for long. She had to move.

Leet turned and sprinted for the other end of the drum stack, reaching it unscathed. He hadn't even fired at her. Perhaps she had incapacitated him.

Her pistol at the ready, she peered around the drum and found him on his knees. One of her wide shots had punctured a drum, releasing a steady stream of liquid. He responded with a burst of half a dozen rounds, all of which flew past her as she retreated behind the drums.

Fuck this! She took off around the other side of the stack, pistol at the high ready. The muzzle of his weapon and a sliver of arm appeared a moment later around the far barrel.

They fired simultaneously, each a single shot that hit home. Sparks flew when Leet's bullet ricocheted off the top of his weapon and traveled on into his arm, eliciting a cry of surprise and pain as it drove him backward away from the drums. The world's toughest hornet stung her at the same time, right at the belt line on her right side, just below her vest. The impact spun her sideways; the instant pain nearly blacked her out.

She came to in a couple of moments, turned, and saw him lying flat on his back in a puddle of fluid from the barrel she'd hit. He slowly raised his submachine gun to finish her off. She steadied against a barrel, her aim shaky from the bullet wound, and fired just as he brought his weapon level.

His almost inhuman scream eclipsed all other sound in the vicinity. He floundered in the fluid, dropped his submachine gun, a SIG MPX .357, not for sale to the public. His screaming intensified when he jerked his head up and caught a glimpse of the hole in the crotch of his pants. His gray head dropped back into the puddle, acknowledgment of Leet's victory by involuntary castration.

Leet felt the blood starting to soak her jeans front and back as she advanced, pain howling up her spine and battering her brain as she staggered forward. She reached him, calmly put the dot in her sight firmly between his eyes, just above that aquiline, patrician nose. Those eyes were closed; he didn't even notice her. The fluid—acetone from the smell of it—had soaked his urban camo tactical suit.

A bullet was too good for him—too neat, too quick. Leet had quit smoking but still carried a lighter with her everywhere, just as other former smokers kept one last pack of unopened cigarettes to steel their willpower. "Never know when you might need one." She barely heard her own words as she found the Zippo in her pocket.

She opened it with a finger snap, high school bathroom style, and sparked it to life with a flick of her index finger. After backing off a few feet, she tossed the flaming lighter into the puddle, turned, and tried to run.

She managed a loping hobble. Every fall of her right foot produced a sword stab of agony. *I wish I could watch you burn, asshole!* She had to settle for listening to his ululating wail as the fire consumed him, melting the skin and fat from his body.

A minor explosion echoed down from the second level. The fire raged behind her as she navigated the warehouse obstacles.

"Margaret!" Shai called from beneath the forklift.

"Go..." It amazed her how raspy she sounded. "Hide outside. The fire..." She smiled at him, pointed toward the archway as if in a dream, then made for the conveyor belt to the second level, a gentler climb than the stairs.

Fuck, I'm going to die.

She'd scrabbled nearly to the summit of the rubber conveyor, practically on hands and knees, when she heard a familiar laugh.

Then the drums began to explode.

* * *

"I wonder where old Swift is..." Max said it aloud, hoping the creep's big mouth would betray him.

Max lay in cover behind three skids and a busted crate, listening to the fight downstairs. Swift had to be on the upper deck.

Swift spoke in a loud whisper, only possible by amplifying his voice. "Pretty slick, Max, loading that case with—"

I know what you're doing, you fucking ox. A speaker must have been placed somewhere on the upper level, probably wireless and synched with a cell phone. Max was supposed to believe that was Swift's actual location. *Amateur.* Tech just wasn't Swift's thing; vintage guns and killer reptiles occupied all of the limited space in his brain compartment. Aside from Leet shooting it out downstairs and Shai being unaccounted for, Max couldn't have been more pleased; only an idiot staked his life on tactics he obviously hadn't practiced.

Gunfire—semi-auto shots from downstairs followed by a shout of masculine pain—drowned out the rest. Max used it to hide the sound of his movements as he crawled a few feet to new cover.

"Didn't take us long to figure it out," Swift followed up with a grunted chortle. "Can't trust anybody anymore; somebody's always got it in for me. I mean, here I am, just a normal guy, mindin' his own business, and you come along, shoot my gator, kill my old lady, burn my house to the ground, steal all my money. I guess you could say that makes us about even, but you know I don't play by the rules."

Max had a better view from his current vantage point. Fading sunlight still somewhat lit the place through the broken windows, but it grew dimmer by the moment. Soon they'd be playing cat and mouse in the dark. Max wanted to finish Swift before it came to that.

Find his fat ass already!

Though he didn't locate Swift, he saw the next best thing: a faint blue glow emanating from a light on the speaker, positioned against a wall about twenty feet away. Max needed nothing more.

"Too bad about the Marines," Swift whispered on. "You fuckers are supposed to be thick as—"

More gunfire drowned out his words, not that Max had really been listening; he was busy scanning the room, estimating Swift's position by examining the optimum trajectories to kill a man who approached the speaker. Two hiding spots stood out, though Max would have chosen neither. Swift would either be in the rafters behind a massive motor built to power an exhaust fan or behind some crates in the far corner. Crates that Swift had to have maneuvered into position. The second location offered a wide field of fire over and through the junk choking the floorspace, leading Max to believe he'd found him.

Fuck it, only one way to find out.

Max pulled out a fresh magazine for the Saint, set it down next to him for a quick reload after shooting up the crates. He sighted in, confident the 5.56 rounds would easily punch through the rotten wood.

Something landed with a metal clank not three feet away from him. *Fuck!* Max rolled to his left, straight into some junk that stopped his progress.

The grenade exploded. Had it been a frag grenade, he likely would have died, but it was merely a flash-bang, most of its concussive impact blocked by an upset metal shelf. The blast initiated a keening wail in his ears nevertheless, which gave him an instant migraine headache and left him disoriented. He rolled onto his back. When he tried to raise the Saint, he found it had fallen from his grasp.

A gargantuan figure charged at him, hippo legs and sasquatch soles traversing the junk with surprising deftness. Swift liked reptiles for a reason; they burst from dormant to deadly fast at the least provocation with nobody the wiser. He charged from the rear, had been hiding near the catwalk to monitor the approach to those crates as it turned out. If nothing else, Swift was living proof that animal cunning outweighed actual intelligence when it came to combat; he would have died years before otherwise.

But Max didn't have time to feel foolish over falling into his trap. He felt around with his right hand, couldn't locate the Saint. Nearly upon Max, Swift launched his great weight through the air, bowie knife in hand, mouth agape as he emitted a war whoop of victory Max could barely hear.

Max's groping hand found something thin, metallic, and gritty with rust. He raised the two-foot section of threaded rod and jabbed at Swift's face as his nemesis crashed down upon him, shaking the floor and knocking the wind from Max. Even over the wailing in his ears, Max heard Swift's cry of shocked agony when the rod found his left eye. Swift instinctively dropped the knife and covered his injured eye with his hands.

Though Swift writhed atop him in pain, neither man had the advantage. Max could barely breathe, every inhalation a struggle as Swift's oppressive bulk constricted his lungs. Swift's partial blindness was only temporary, for Max had failed to jab the rod through his eyeball.

Max smashed him in the temple with the rod, opening a nasty laceration, then followed up by jabbing the rod into his throat. That did the trick. Swift rolled partway off him. Max shoved him the rest of the way, freeing himself. He sat up, cracked Swift across the bridge of his nose with the rod as further insult and injury.

With Swift incapacitated, Max fought to catch his breath. He didn't have time to find the Saint, however. Swift would recover quickly; for all Max knew he might be playing possum. The only way to predict his next move was to rob him of it before it happened. Max drew his Glock, put an immobilizing knee on Swift's chest. With his left hand, Max grabbed Swift's injured throat and held the gun to his head with the right.

"What were you saying, Carter?" Max said. "I didn't catch that part about the Marines." *But I think I got the gist of it.*

"Go ahead, kill me," Swift rasped. "Won't save any of you. We win again. We always win."

Leet's voice reached him through the dusty air, though he couldn't make out her words. Past the catwalk, the final rays of sunshine illuminated swirling clouds of smoke building at the ceiling. The gunfire had ceased.

"I love your optimism, Swift." Max stared into his unblinking blue eye. "But otherwise you're a piece of shit. When you get to hell, give that cow you married my regards."

Blood spattered Max's face before he even heard the gunshot. The pain hit him in the next instant, an intense, dizzying pulse from his right forearm. The bullet had passed right through. Max still held his pistol, but the new shooter had him covered.

Ben stepped forward from the shadows. He'd likely accessed the building via the second-floor entrance, a rickety flight of stairs on the building's exterior. *Too many fucking entrances to this place.*

"Cavalry's here!" Ben announced, his winning smile winking in near darkness. If not for the body armor bulging out of his pinpoint Oxford dress shirt and the pistol he trained on Max's head, he would have looked like a model in the L.L. Bean catalog. "Can you believe this, Max? *Never* send a merc to do a Marine's job."

"Semper fi? You're not faithful to anyone. You're no Marine in my book," Max growled through clenched teeth, his pain excruciating.

Ben laughed. "Well, you don't get to write this book, Max. Winners write history, while pawns like you wind up in shallow graves. Now drop the weapon."

"You mind if I kill this fat sack of snake shit before you waste me? What good is he to you? He'll shoot you in the back to take your cut the moment he gets the chance."

Ben shrugged. "Eh, he has his uses. Hell, he's living proof that the Agency and the Bureau can work together! Swift and I are about to be very rich men, once we take this kid apart and figure out what makes him tick. But don't worry, I'll whistle taps in your honor after we bury you." He laughed again, the hearty guffaw of a nabob sipping a martini after a successful afternoon on the golf course. "Now toss the—"

An explosion rocked the warehouse, quickly followed by another. The blasts shook the floor, clouding the air with dust that rained down from the rafters.

Swift wasted no time seizing the moment, as well as Max's bleeding right forearm. Pain burned white-hot behind Max's eyelids for an instant, and the pistol dropped from his hand. Swift pulled Max's arm, simultaneously raising both knees and rolling in a reverse tumble that propelled Max off him.

Bullets cracked through the air past Max as Ben tried to finish him. Everything had become a hazy target at best in the swirling dust and falling darkness. Max heard Ben shout in surprise and perhaps pain, followed by a tongue lashing from Leet.

Then Swift was on him, knife in hand once again, foregoing his guns, nice and personal. Max had no problem with that. He rolled to the side, avoiding the first knife thrust, and sprang to his feet. Swift, deceivingly quick as always, jumped to his feet and slashed at him, the blade passing just shy of Max's throat.

"Fail!" Max said.

He chortled as he drove the toe of his boot into Swift's knee. He followed with a solid left hammer blow that landed just ahead of his ear, buying Max enough breathing room to draw his Ka-Bar. Backpedaling would be impossible for either of them without some piece of junk snagging a foot. Max preferred it that way. *Try to run this time!*

The back of his mind acknowledged the gun battle in progress between Leet and Ben, but none of it truly registered with him. Swift had his undivided attention. The pain in his arm even deserted him, yielding beneath numbing shots of adrenaline.

They squared off, each man conscious of the chance he might trip in the debris. Max angled to Swift's left to stay on his blind side. He would have preferred to take the defensive and wait on the fat sack of shit to make the first move, but he didn't have that luxury. Swift still had a pistol, might say fuck it and decide to use it at any moment. Max moved in, led with a left-handed punch that missed, followed by a knife slash for the neck that wound up grazing Swift's plate carrier, slashing through to the ceramic plate. Swift responded with a quick step forward, closing to within grappling distance. Spinning to the side, Max evaded his knife attack and likewise avoided tying up with him. The last thing he wanted was the knife fight turning into a wrestling match, one he was certain to lose.

They turned, slashed, stabbed, feinted. Max scored first blood, burying the Ka-Bar deep into Swift's right shoulder before ripping it out hard with a rending slash. Despite his high pain threshold, the gushing wound left Swift growling. He lashed out like the wounded animal he'd become, slashing with his right arm, trying to grab Max's knife wrist with his left hand. But Max had put a true hurting on his knife arm. A profuse amount of blood pulsed from the wound to trickle down in erratic red rivers, slowing Swift down, making him more frantic to save his life.

And then, like the coward he was deep at heart, Swift exited the fight by leaping over some toppled shelving, miraculously planting his feet on two tiny sections of clear floor. The knife in his hand prevented him from pulling the Model 1911 .45 holstered at his belt on the right side, so he wouldn't be able to get a shot in but he could improvise. With his free left hand, he yanked his last flash-bang from his plate carrier, pulled the pin with the thumb of his knife hand, and tossed.

Max dove into the clutter, extended his left arm and smacked the grenade back at him before it hit the floor. Pain returned when he landed hard on his right arm atop a section of filthy fiberglass insulation, some bum's bedding, that somewhat cushioned his fall. The grenade popped somewhere over Max's head, its brief flash of fire singing his clothing and the back of his head, the concussion deafening and disorienting.

Max lay on his stomach for several seconds in a hazy daze of pain and ringing ears. Though he could hear nothing, he saw Swift clearly enough, lying a few feet away. His clothing smoldered; his face bore third-degree burns, and his tolerance for pain had folded. If the grenade blast hadn't temporarily deafened Max, the agonized cries from Swift's gaping maw likely would have.

But even wounded and broken down, Swift remained a threat. Max spotted him reaching for the .45 on his belt, ready to take Max down with him. Stepping over a rotted cardboard box of moldering documents, Max brought down his heel on Swift's forearm, stomping three times until he retracted his hand from the vicinity of his pistol.

Max knelt next to him, put the Ka-Bar's cold steel against his fat, wrinkled throat, hoping he could feel it.

"Do it," Swift rasped. "And I will see you in Hell."

Even if Swift could have heard him, Max had no final farewell for the overgrown, feeble-minded murderer who had failed at both herpetology and mercenary work. That Swift knew he'd met his maker at Max's hand was consolation enough. He stabbed him in the throat as opposed to a clean slash, content to let his old nemesis and occasional partner bleed out slowly. Though it could never happen slowly enough to match the suffering Max still lived with.

With his other weapons lost in the jumble of wreckage, Max drew Swift's .45 and turned to survey the situation. Ben knelt atop Leet, her back pinned to the deck on the catwalk, the two silhouetted by the raging fire behind them. Leet barely managed to keep his weapon turned away from her. Max aimed for Ben, trying to get a clear shot over the iron sights on Swift's pistol.

Shai appeared at Ben's back, and Max staid his trigger finger. He charged through the wreckage to save Shai, who grabbed Ben by the collar of his body armor and flung him off Leet, sending him tumbling a few feet down the catwalk.

Max fell forward when his toe caught on something, his wound announcing itself again when he landed. When he again looked up, Shai knelt over Ben, who lay with his pistol raised between them.

"No!" Max shouted an instant before Ben fired.

The bullet struck Shai high in the chest. The impact spun him around and propelled him into the catwalk railing. But Shai didn't fall. Ben fired again, his shot throwing up sparks when it rang off the railing next to Shai's head. Unable to get a good bead on Ben from this angle, Max held his fire and advanced. He could take no chances with Shai standing downrange.

Ben tried to roll to his feet, only to be stopped when Shai descended on him with outstretched arms. He fired once at Shai's head, missing, before pistol whipping the boy above his ear. Shai didn't bleed of course, but the synthetic skin below his cropped hair parted to expose the composite metal beneath.

Shai barely flinched at the blow. Showing no sign of rage, no sign of pain, he reached down and seized Ben by the throat. Ben fired again, hitting nothing. He then cried out once, very faintly, before Shai ripped out his trachea with bare hands.

Max stood dumbfounded by what he'd just witnessed. His hearing had returned, though his head still ached as though he'd recently awoken from an all-night bender.

He should have moved faster, for another man then appeared on the catwalk and tried to attack Shai with a stun baton. Shai dodged the thrust with a dancer's grace as Max opened fire. His first shot grazed the baton wielder across the side of his head; the second cleanly missed when the man turned and fled for the stairs. Max reached the catwalk just in time to glimpse the man's bald head and flapping shirttail as he fled through the archway to the railroad loading dock. The fire had spread over most of the floor, feeding on the trash and clutter. The bald man had barely escaped past the flames.

"Dammit!" Max then realized he had bigger problems to worry about: Shai's damaged covering; the roaring fire, producing toxic smoke that completely obscured the rafters, the gray cloud slowly descending; and Leet, who lay a few feet away bleeding heavily from a shot she'd taken just below her body armor. Max ran to her.

"I got him!" She gasped for air. "That piece of shit killed Don." Ben must have pistol whipped her at some point, for she also bled from a laceration on her scalp.

Max offered her a forced smile. "So did I, but we'll celebrate later. We need to go."

Shai and Max got Leet upright, only to find she could no longer walk after losing so much blood. She'd already turned pale. Soon she'd assume that familiar shade of purplish blue that Max had no desire to see.

Max picked her up as gently as he could, his forearm burning in pain as he slung her over his shoulder. He made for the second-floor exit as the toxic cloud finally descended upon them. Gagging on the smoke pouring out of the doorway, Max didn't pause to wonder whether the rusting stairway would hold the combined weight of himself and Leet. The journey down the steel risers was slow and perilous, yet nothing gave way before they made it to the ground.

Shai took the lead, and Max didn't have a problem with that. *Could I have ripped out Ben's throat with my bare hands?* He highly doubted it. Shai could obviously protect himself. Any thugs stalking the back alleys in search of easy prey would get far more than they'd bargained for if they fucked with him. *Too bad Daniel had to keep his strength a secret.*

Several explosions resembling an artillery barrage rumbled. With a tremendous flashover, the warehouse collapsed in their wake. Max glanced backward. A hazy, warm light resembling a new dawn rose above the rooftops. The column of smoke could be seen for miles. He heard distant sirens wailing as firetrucks raced to the scene.

Fortunately, no one had located and stripped the Suburban in their absence. Max and Shai loaded Leet, now unconscious, into the back seat. The boy stayed with her, applying pressure to her wound with the combat dressing Max provided.

Finished with the fight and free of carrying Leet, Max's adrenaline subsided, allowing his pain the freedom to roam once more. Blood soaked the lower sleeve of his ruined jacket. He wiped his right hand, slick with blood, on his trousers. They had morphed into post-apocalyptic beings, perfectly at home in the surrounding neighborhood.

"How's she look?" Max asked as he pulled onto the street.

"Not good but she's still alive."

"I think we can get her to the hospital in time. Don't worry; everything will be all right." He didn't realize the absurdity of telling an android not to worry until after he'd said it.

"No," Shai responded softly. "It will never be all right."

17

Filthy, bloodied, reeking of soot, clothes in tatters, Max stood out even in a DC hospital, where personnel saw all manner of gruesome injuries during their shifts.

"Damn, when did World War III start?" a male nurse asked of a female counterpart as he watched Max and Shai approach the nurses' station.

"It's over already; you missed it," Max teased, trying to lighten the mood. Bad enough that he looked frightening; acting the part would never get them in to see Leet.

"Sir, the emergency room is on the first floor," said the female nurse. "Call for a wheelchair," she said to her coworker. Closely eyeballing Max, she added, "Extra-large."

"No need for that. I've already been there." Max showed them his right arm, the gunshot wound freshly disinfected and bandaged. "We're here to see Margaret Leet. Is she out of surgery yet?"

"Are you a relative?" the female nurse skeptically queried.

"I'm her brother, Michael Adams." He motioned to Shai. "This is her son."

The female nurse, obviously the higher-ranking of the two, asked, "ID?"

Max handed her his phony Nevada driver's license. He prepared to recite the same bullshit story he'd told in the ER: they'd taken a wrong turn and driven into a street shootout between rival gangs. His tale hadn't even raised an eyebrow in the ER, so common were such events in DC. While scrubbing his bullet wound, the weary doctor said, "We'll notify the police, but don't expect them anytime soon. You'll probably have to submit a report at the station."

The nurse gave his ID only a cursory glance before handing it back. "Let's see…" She tapped some keys and consulted a monitor. "Leet, Margaret… room sixteen. They brought her up half an hour ago. I'll need you to sign in."

"Not a problem." Max took the clipboard and inked his Michael Adams.

"Good thing the boy wasn't with you," said the male nurse, holding out a lollipop to the kid.

"Yeah. We were on our way to pick him up." Shai had changed clothes in the car, dropping his post-apocalyptic zombie guise. He looked a little odd in the baggy hooded sweatshirt he'd donned to cover his damaged head and body, but uninjured people didn't attract much attention around here. Had Shai been of adult stature, the nurse wouldn't even have noticed him.

Shai declined the lollipop offered by the male nurse.

Max led him to room sixteen, nearly colliding with a doctor exiting the room, who upon viewing Max curtly informed him that only family could visit. So Max showed his ID and delivered the same story.

"Yes," Leet called from her bed, drawing out the word, still a bit loopy from anesthesia. "That's my boy."

Any doubts the doctor might have had were erased.

Shai darted past the doctor and ran to her bedside. He took her hand. Above a delirious half-smile, tears formed in Leet's eyes.

"I brought you something, Mar—Mom." From the pocket of his hoodie, Shai produced a short-stemmed white rose and presented it to her. Max could only surmise that Shai had bought it from a peddler while his bullet hole was being cleansed.

Tears ran freely down Leet's cheeks as she accepted the gift, the sort of panacea a jaded doctor working at an inner-city hospital could never supply.

"How's her condition?" Max asked the doctor.

"Stable. The bullet nicked the large intestine, but fortunately no major blood vessels were struck. She received four pints of blood and will likely feel weak for several days, but she'll be good as new after a couple weeks. Infection is our biggest concern now that she's stabilized, but we've started her on some antibiotics."

Max thanked him and entered the room. He kept back from the bed however, not wishing to intrude on Leet and Shai. Her mission was over; she didn't need a reminder that his remained active. And that he currently had no idea how to proceed.

He needn't have worried about upsetting Leet. Her eyelids drooped after a couple of minutes of woozy banter with Shai. Soon she fell asleep, the white rose clutched in her hand.

Max closed the drapes, shutting out a brilliant dawn. Shai remained by Leet, and Max didn't interrupt them. He pulled up a worn vinyl chair and sat. Twenty-four sleepless hours and two intense battles quickly caught up to him. He fell into a deep and thankfully dreamless sleep.

He awakened with a start, checked his watch: 1045. A dull ache radiated from every muscle, joint, and organ in his body. His right arm felt stiff, and it hurt when he flexed his hand. He would only shake it off if he got moving. *Yeah... but to where?*

"Has she been awake at all?" Max asked.

Shai gave a small shake of his head. "No. I don't think she will awaken for a while."

"We need to go, let her continue to rest."

"I know. I don't want to go, but you're right." How could an android look so forlorn?

"She'll be fine. But you might be in danger still."

After a few moments Shai said, "I'll always be in danger, Max. I'll always be a danger."

That comment took Max aback. "Why do you say that?" Once more he envisioned Shai ripping Ben's throat out. *But that's not it.*

"Dynamite. Television. The internet."

Max had a brief laugh. "Not sure I follow you, pal."

"Each was a radical invention created for the betterment of mankind." He kissed Leet's hand, then turned to face Max. "Their inventors created them for peaceful purposes. But they have been used to subjugate humanity instead, the noble intentions of benevolent creators twisted into instruments of murder and mass control by malicious opportunists. The wisest and kindest of intentions don't matter when greed and narcissism become involved."

"I wish I could find fault with your point."

"I have been alive—if you wish to call it that—for less than four years. My father programmed me with what you might call encyclopedic knowledge. Science, mathematics, history, two-dozen foreign languages; he left out nothing that he could possibly squeeze into my memory. On a human scale, my IQ is well over 200, but that measurement is fairly meaningless for a mind like mine. But that's nothing; it's not what those pursuing us are interested in. My mnemonic programming is what matters. Just as a human brain records everything its possessor witnesses, so does mine. As my memory fills, older memories of insignificant nature are automatically erased, therefore having no impact on my actions, my thoughts, or the decisions

I make. Humans simply forget, even things they wish to remember, and are influenced by things they wish to forget."

The boy stopped, as if caught in a moment of self-consciousness. "My apologies. I am not being boastful, nor am I trying to bore you."

Max chuckled. "I never thought that. And you certainly never bore me."

"But I should come to my point, nevertheless. I spent most of my existence in my father's lab, where my knowledge lay dormant as he perfected me. Having this knowledge means nothing, however, unless the possessor can use it to promote the greater good. Otherwise, it is simply a curse.

"I realized this even before being thrust into the world of human beings. My father's best friend, a close colleague who contributed to my physical construction, betrayed him to Mossad and forced us to flee Israel. That was my first experience of being baffled, for my father programmed me with no knowledge regarding the human nature of good and evil. In truth that cannot be programmed; the duality of man can only be experienced and evaluated firsthand."

Max nodded. "That's one hell of an introduction to the ways of mankind. But there are exceptional people in this world, Shai. I've been privileged to know a few." *Most of whom are dead.* "Don't allow the wicked to poison you against the rest of us. Men like Ben Fisher and Swift Carter are the aberrations."

Shai stared at Max for several moments. "Would you have said the same about Mr. Fisher three days ago?"

"No. I never thought he would betray me."

"It is the nature of human beings, Max. A dangerous minority of men will always do whatever it takes to become richer and more powerful. The latter position is the most dangerous. The powerful can never be sated, thus they constantly strive to acquire more power. Every step up the ladder only impels them to take another. Along the way they not only destroy lives but find better, more efficient means of destruction. It is never enough.

"The high explosives invented for blasting through mountains soon became landmines and artillery shells. Radio and television were immediately commandeered by the powerful to brainwash the masses with propaganda, driving mindless nationalism while simultaneously destroying human decency. The internet is the greatest tool for communication ever invented. It could have united people the world over; instead it has built walls and dug moats between nations, neighbors, relatives.

"All because of powerful men who never wish to see unity amongst their perceived inferiors. There is no profit in unity. There are vast sums to be amassed through warfare however, and for these men there is never enough."

Max took a moment to digest all he said. "I agree. I've been wrapped up in the military-industrial complex for most of my adult life, lured in by the promise of serving something greater than myself. I thought I was working for the good guys. Perhaps I was sometimes, but most times I wasn't so sure. Those illusions flew out the window for good when the CIA murdered my family. But honestly, I should have seen it sooner. The more research I do, the more I realize the truth has always been there in plain sight. Just stare past the cardboard cutouts of politicians and the shimmering screen of bullshit.

"Otherwise, I have no regrets. As much as I've hated working for the strong arm of the US government, better I do it than someone else. I like to think I have the temperament for it. Morally bankrupt men may call most of the shots, but I've never flinched from telling them to go to hell. The last thing the world needs are yes men and self-serving leeches doing my sort of work. God knows there are enough of them already."

"I don't know your history, Max, but from what I've seen of your character, I can only surmise that you have done your share of good in this world."

Despite his effort at a grin for the kind words, Max grimaced. "I wish I could agree with you. But I still try, and I'm not done just yet."

"I hope not, because I remain in need of your services."

Max hesitated in responding. *How many promises have you made?* Too many to count and most never delivered upon. But again, he had always tried. "I'll get you to safety, Shai. Somehow." He unleashed an exasperated chuckle. "And please don't ask me how."

"There is no need to ask how. I can think of no one better suited to the task."

"Well, we've gotten this far. I think I can take you a few more miles, get you to someone who can properly shelter you until this mess blows over."

"It will never blow over, Max. Not while they can still get ahold of me. I am explosives, television, and the internet all in a single unit. You foiled the plans of a few men who wished to capitalize by selling my secrets to the powerful. But it cannot go on forever. One day I'll be taken—torn apart, retooled, perverted into their next weapon of mass control and destruction. A handful of people like you and Margaret will never be enough to stop them.

"And sadly, due to my ability to think and learn, I may one day succumb to the basest of human temptations, with no prodding from outside forces. I felt something different when I saw someone about to kill Margaret. My father never programmed me to feel rage. For those same reasons, he didn't program me to be nonviolent, mistakenly believing it would never be an issue. My father was as much an optimist as a cynic, and he hoped he could spare me from the worst of mankind. And yet I believe I felt rage in that moment.

"I don't want to feel that way ever again. After killing Fisher, I sensed a minute change in my thought patterns. I may grow to enjoy violence, as some humans do. And rage on my behalf, coupled with servitude to a malicious government, could spell the end of humanity."

Max sat dumbstruck in the sticky vinyl chair for quite some time. "We'll assimilate you into society. I'll take you back to Otto, see if he can repair your skin. And I know other people—good people—who might be willing to adopt you and teach you and love you like a son."

"Max, I appreciate your noble intentions, but it won't work. The human race isn't ready for me yet, though I hope that one day that time will come. I cannot profane my father's memory by becoming either an instrument of evil or a prototype for one. I hope you realize why I cannot remain here, even as I hope that you might help me. You are the only man I know who possesses the will to accomplish this. I would do it myself, but my programming forbids it."

Shai said no more.

Max fell silent as well. Shai reminded him so much of David, the son he had lost. If it were possible to keep Shai's identity a secret, he would have look after the boy himself. Unfortunately, Shai was correct in all he had said. *His secret is out. There's no other way.* Still Max had no desire to act as the hand of God that would smite from existence the greatest marvel ever produced by man. *But if not me, then who?*

Leet wasn't about to do it, even if she were presently capable. Though she'd dropped all delusions regarding her pals at the FBI, she would still attempt to hide Shai in the mistaken belief that she could hold the world's malevolent forces at bay. *And the cycle will continue until they finally get to him.*

Max stood. "Wake Margaret up. She'll want to see you before you go."

***

Famished, feeling like he'd been beaten mercilessly with a phone book, Max stopped by the gift shop on the hospital's first floor.

"What'll it be?" he asked Shai as he reached into the drink cooler for a bottle of diet Mountain Dew. Though Shai didn't need food or drink, Max had seen him partake of both and wondered if he had any favorites.

"Just apple juice, please. Soda corrodes my insides."

"You and me both." He grabbed a couple of pre-packaged subs, mostly bread with a couple scraps of meat thrown in, and a small container of cottage cheese to delude himself into believing this was a healthy meal.

On the way to checkout, Max spied several rabbits scattered amongst various stuffed animals on a shelf. He hadn't paid much attention to Shai's lost rabbit but supposed that long ears were resemblance enough. "What do you think? They look pretty close."

"Hmm…" Shai picked through the animals, scrutinized the rabbits until he found one he liked. "This one. He's just like Bao."

Max laughed. "I think so too."

The rabbit took both their minds off of what would happen later. They basked in the comforting moment, a safe place they could never dwell again. For David, that security had been a stuffed dog that brought him comfort when his father was away. In the end though, the stuffed animal wasn't enough to replace a father always gone.

As they drove away from the hospital, Shai said, "There is something I need to do before… Well, you know."

"Okay." One did not deny a final request from a friend. "What is it?"

"I need to do someone a favor. I'll need a laptop and reliable wi-fi access."

"On it." There was a big-box bookstore with a wi-fi hotspot not far from the storage unit, which he had to visit anyway. He'd washed up a bit in the hospital room before leaving, but he needed to change clothes. The rags he wore now were only suitable for burning.

He departed the unit freshly dressed in black t-shirt and jeans below a summer sport jacket he'd donned to look semi-respectable. He felt evil carrying the can of gasoline and well-worn shovel out to the Suburban. *I've buried shit with this shovel but never gold.*

Outside the realm of covert and ruthless government operations, the civilian world continued about its daily business. The people surrounding them in the bookstore café sat zombified, most staring at their phone screens, oblivious to the unseen forces controlling their lives. *But are they oblivious? Or simply in a state of denial?* He supposed that either was possible, depending on the person, before dropping the matter from his thoughts.

Shai got busy on Max's laptop, while Max kept a vigilant watch on the customers. Not all of Fisher's pals had died, and he didn't expect the survivors to abandon their relentless chase. They'd probably regrouped already. Perhaps they were close by, even now, waiting for him to carelessly drop his guard.

Max's thoughts drifted to Swift as he observed the comings and goings of the customers. Despite the fate he would deal to Shai, Max should have felt some small measure of satisfaction. Another of his family's killers had died—this time by his own hand—rendered down to an unidentifiable pile of ashes. Yet the revenge he'd exacted on Swift tasted bland in the aftermath; it had gotten him nowhere in the hunt for Jarvis, the mastermind. *Right back at square fucking one.* The scenario seemed to play out the same over and over. *Is this what I have to look forward to? And if I ever do kill Jarvis, will even that be enough to satisfy me?* For the first time, he began to question the motives that drove his quest. Retribution seemed like more of a duty than a desire, let alone the fixation it had been only a few days previously.

Enough. Call it the post-mission blues and shake it off.

But his new and unsettling thoughts on the pointlessness of his quest lingered. He simply couldn't banish them at the moment.

Shai's fingers flew over the keyboard. Max had never seen anyone type so fast, and he could only wonder what sort of favor the kid was working on and for whom. He supposed he could ask, yet he didn't. *It's none of my business unless he makes it so.*

Shai did not reveal the nature of his favor. He said nothing at all for several hours as he incessantly typed and clicked, finally finishing up at around 1700. "I hope the recipient of that favor appreciates the effort you put into it," Max said as they packed up his laptop and prepared to hit the road.

Shai shrugged. "I'm not so sure that I do. But that isn't up to me."

18

Less than a year before, Max had journeyed to DC for answers that might only be provided by a select few agents of various status within the CIA. He received no help from them for his trouble, only their cold and mutilated corpses after they refused to yield any significant leads. After the interrogations came the inevitable cleanup. He sunk one body in Baltimore harbor, and he buried the other two in an old landfill located in a tract of lonely Maryland woods with all the other trash.

Shai would not be resting beside killers. He deserved better.

As Max turned the sandy earth with the shovel—pain shooting up his right arm with every jab and scoop of the spade—he considered the spot he'd chosen: a low rise in the coastal marshes of Virginia, not far from Quantico. He'd visited the spot only once, some twenty years before, when Janet came for his graduation from the Basic School. They found it while taking a hike and were so moved by the wild beauty of the place, with its commanding view of the primeval marshes, that they'd made love in this very spot. It seemed like an eternity ago. Deer and other wildlife were the only regular visitors here. He knew a dozen other spots that offered greater isolation. Yet he knew of none more suitable for a final resting place.

The drudgery of the dig absorbed him. He threw himself into the work with a great and tireless vigor, the pain in his arm be damned.

***

You understand now.

At first Shai's thoughts had come with no perspective at all, for they had been rudimentary, the parroting of requests and assignments from his father, tasks carried out by a device made to carry out tasks: *Read this and try to memorize it, word for word. Find the shape that doesn't fit the pattern. Study this treatise and attempt to analyze it.*

Now they came in the second person yet still in his father's voice. *You cannot be afraid. This is impossible.*

No, Father, I am afraid right now. The thought came, for the first time, in a strange inner voice he recognized as his own, startling him even though it shouldn't have. Illogic had begun to take control, overriding the coding installed by his father… or perhaps merely cooperating with it. A computer could not think, only do what it was commanded to. The benefits of actual thought—the ability to create and solve problems independent of commands and programming—came with a price: fear, sorrow, rage, and a host of other emotions.

As Shai watched the gently lapping water in the cove turn ever brighter shades of gold while the sun set behind his back, he finally understood exactly why the world was such an imperfect place, despite having in abundance all the ingredients necessary for a utopia. And as endless night descended on what might be referred to as his life, he likewise comprehended the misery pervasive throughout the world—for he had learned to feel it.

The first seed of what he came to recognize as emotion had been attachment, first to his father and then to Margaret. He hadn't understood why he desired this, though he now recognized it as a reaction to a fear he hadn't known and could not comprehend until he saw Don gunned down in the restroom. *I was terrified.*

When creating Shai, his father had never have imagined him being able to feel emotions, even in the best of circumstances, and Shai had a hard time believing it even now. In the wake of those early blips of feeling, his programming quickly took control once again, balancing his thoughts and always returning them to logic. Yet as his feelings multiplied, the logic keeping them in check began to diminish, abandoning him for longer periods to the unpredictable tides of human emotion.

Though he knew it no longer mattered—that soon he would cease to exist—a single question continued to batter the core of his thought processes: *Is emotion really such a terrible thing?* After all, it had been his emotions—loyalty, anger, affection—that saved Margaret from Fisher, not his programmed code that directed him to be benevolent to humans at all times. Emotion had made him realize that people were not all the same, that not all of humanity was worth saving. Some, indeed, had to be eliminated for the greater good, for their purposes centered only on destruction.

That last notion disturbed him the most, for it resembled the hateful thoughts of an indoctrinated zealot. Who was he—or anyone else for that matter—to decide whether men should live or die? Could such condemnations be logical, or were they always the product of hatred and distrust? Despite the lessons of history, many in the world still wished to see those harboring different ideologies cast down, imprisoned, put to death, just for thinking differently. *They will not admit it, but the thoughts are there, and all driven by emotion. And if my emotions should ever wrest total control from logic, I could become just like them.*

This could not be allowed to happen. Despite their worst feelings, most of humanity lacked the resources to act upon them. They could only follow. Shai could take command. And quite easily. Just one emotionally driven, misguided thought on his behalf could throw the world into utter chaos.

Many emotions, however, had not visited him; he only knew them by definition. Chief among them, the hardest to comprehend, was regret. *A sense of loss, disappointment, or dissatisfaction.* Despite all of the hate and suffering he'd witnessed during a very short period, he felt no regret for having been created. For in addition to seeing the worst humans could do, he had also seen them at their best.

He missed Margaret's presence the instant he left her. *Do I love her, as a human child naturally loves its mother?* He couldn't tell, though he knew that his feelings for her surpassed simple preference.

His thoughts turned to Max, who toiled in a pit, not fifty feet away, back in the pines. *He is a good man, even if he doubts it himself.* For that very reason, Shai couldn't help but fear for his future. *If he finds the men he seeks, if he exacts his revenge, will his regret be sated? Will he have any further purpose in life after that? Will he simply end his own existence, having nothing else to fight for?* Shai couldn't say. Not only because it was impossible to predict the future in anything other than broad terms, but because Max Ahlgren remained something of an enigma, even to an intelligence like Shai's. Put simply, Max was no normal human, despite the fact that he possessed the entire array of human emotions. Shai considered him nothing short of extraordinary.

And that is what the world needs, for despite my intelligence I cannot fix society. That is the task and duty of extraordinary people. Margaret Leet, Max Ahlgren, and others like them were the only ones capable of saving humanity from itself.

I can only wish them luck and infinite courage. They will need both.

***

Max speared the shovel into the dirt pile before swiping at the gritty sweat on his brow with a dirt-streaked forearm. "It's time, Shai."

Shai sat with his back turned to Max as he watched the sun set for the last time. He nodded and then stood. Max took his hand and led him into the stand of pines and scrub. Soon they stood next to Shai's grave.

This is not right, Max thought as he looked down on the boy. *What kind of world do we live in where intelligence like this winds up buried in a hole?* Meanwhile, a pack of ruthless wolves would continue to run society their way—through indoctrination, intimidation, extortion, genocide. *All the good he could have done, a savior cut down before he could even scratch a mark on the world.*

"Before I go, I have something to tell you," Shai said.

"I'm listening."

"The favor I did today was for you."

"I don't deserve it, whatever it is."

"That will be for you to decide once you see it." He offered Max a wan grin. "I was constructed with highly advanced software that records the facial telemetry of everyone I see. Today I entered the data of the man who escaped from the warehouse and conducted a search for his identity. You will find his information in an email I sent to your dark web address. I believe he is connected with the death of your family. I hope this helps you in whatever you are after."

"Thank you. I hope so too, though right now I feel like following you into that hole."

"Please do not do that. Just remember, if this person is involved in your family's murder, killing him will not bring them back to life. And if you are successful in bringing them all to justice, please promise me that you will stop there."

"I will. I promise."

"You must miss your son terribly." Shai patted the back of Max's hand in an attempt at comfort.

"Every moment of the day. He was the best of me."

"Thank you for doing this. I know it is horrible for you. I'm scared."

Max heaved a sigh. "So am I. Do you remember when I told you that you're more of a man than most men?"

"Yes."

"It's the truth. And all men face this moment in the end."

"I am ready."

I am not. But that didn't matter. Duty—and loyalty—trumped any feelings of apprehension. He stepped behind Shai and drew his pistol.

***

Max held a desiccated pine bough over the lighter's flame, watched as the reddish-brown needles started to crackle and smoke. The flames climbed up the branch, and when the bough was nicely alight, he tossed it into the grave. With one dull whoosh the gasoline ignited, flames shooting upward from the hole. A noisome stench of burning plastic and frying electronics soon permeated the smoky air.

"I'll make the most of what you've given me, even if it won't bring them back." He thought of Swift and the miniscule measure of satisfaction he felt now that the man was dead. *It doesn't matter. It's all about duty, same as this.* And at least this duty was done. The Nexus project had perished, though eventually some scientist would pick up where Daniel Farber left off. Max only hoped that humanity could handle the next android marvel thrust into the world.

The acrid black smoke produced by Shai's burning skin soon overpowered Max. As he stepped away, he noticed the stuffed rabbit lying on the ground about a foot from the pit. He quickly snatched it up, then backed away from the intense heat. As much as he missed David, he hadn't kept any of his belongings—looking upon them after his death had been far too painful. The photos, which he rarely looked at, were hard enough to endure.

Shai had developed emotions to a point that Max wondered if he also had a soul. "If you do, say hello to David. I think you guys will get along."

He tossed the rabbit into the flames, then sat back against a tree to watch the fire roar.

19

Max drove north on Route 1 filled with a sense of utter despondency. Parting with comrades who had fallen during a mission was never easy, but the soldiers he'd worked with had signed on for war, and the responsibility for their deaths always rested in their own cold fingers. Even Heat, a civilian, had known the danger, though Max doubted she'd truly grasped its magnitude until she lay dying.

But Shai had never been given a choice. He had been created to improve the world and revolutionize how we thought about life itself. *I wish it could have ended differently. He might have fulfilled his purpose.* But Max doubted he would have been allowed the chance. As a believer in free will, he couldn't have denied Shai his last request. *The call wasn't mine in the end.* Yet the question would always remain: Could Shai have beaten the odds and changed the world for the better?

I'll wrestle with that question for the rest of my days.

Max had dreaded the possibility of Shai's death since his initial surprise at having to guard him. From babies to adolescents, enough child corpses already capered about in his nightmares. He would dream of Shai as well, no question. But he wouldn't be playing with the other children. They had died senselessly, casualties of war or the treachery of government organizations, while Shai had perished willingly and for a noble cause, as much a good soldier as a lost innocent. Max knew he would always blame himself for Shai's untimely demise, even though the boy had absolved him of all responsibility. *Doesn't matter. I pulled the trigger.*

Technically, Max's assigned mission was over—he'd seen Shai safely to his only logical end. But now he had to consider what might have befallen Leet since his departure. They hadn't slain all of the agents after Nexus, and the survivors—Green from the safehouse and the mysterious figure spotted at the warehouse—would still be hunting for Shai. They'd had time to regroup and formulate a plan, and Leet was in no position to stop them. Max pondered how they would go about seizing her. *Arrest warrant, probably.* He didn't think they would kill her, not yet, but they might well have snatched her from the hospital already, either legally or by abduction.

If she was still there, she would certainly be under surveillance.

Max had to spring her from the hospital somehow so they could disappear for a while and work on clearing their names. Marklin could help with that. One of the general's clients, Senator Pierce, still owed Max a favor. But he needed breathing room before he could make the call.

He needed a plan right now, yet nothing occurred to him as he drove. Then he saw a sign for a shopping complex looming ahead, America's largest retailer of general household goods topping the display. Rudiments of a strategy clicked together in his mind. Max considered the goods he might need to pull off a disguise and a distraction as he drove into the lot. Fireworks stood out as a necessity, provided they could be legally purchased in Virginia. If not, he could improvise with certain goods from his storage unit, though overkill would be an understatement for that.

* * *

Upon reaching the hospital, Max made straight for the priority parking area near the ER entrance, reserved for police, emergency responders, and hospital security vehicles. A lowered security gate, operated by a guard in a shelter, barred access to the lot. Max drove past the lot, hung a left, and scrutinized the vehicles parked there as he slowly cruised by. Five cars occupied the twenty-odd spaces: a DC squad car, two white Jeep Cherokees topped with yellow strobe lights, and two black vehicles, one a Suburban and the other a Crown Vic. Both the black cars sported government plates. Hardly confirmation that agents were guarding Leet—government vehicles moved about DC like ants on a carcass at any hour of the day—but perhaps an indicator. The police cruiser might have been there for the same reason.

Max drove on, circling the complex as he tried to figure out which room on the third floor Leet occupied. He tried to picture the labyrinth of corridors, though it proved hard to remember. When last he'd been here, getting Leet to the ER and himself patched up had been his only priorities. He hadn't noticed much of anything else. *Think.* He retraced the steps he'd taken to reach the third floor from the first-floor ER. *That side of the building.* Or so he hoped…

He pulled into a space between two cars, facing the hospital, and shut off the engine. His binoculars lay ready on the passenger seat. Hospitals never slept but people did. The dashboard clock read 2:36 am, and most of the windows were dark. Max believed that one of the two illuminated rooms on the third floor housed Leet. He focused the binoculars and watched, waited. Agents on watch would be bored, perhaps pacing the room, yet he saw no silhouettes moving between the slight part in the curtains during almost half an hour of surveillance.

Maybe I got it wrong. He switched to the other room, where the curtains were wider apart. After a few minutes he made out the shoulders of a figure moving about. He couldn't be sure, but he thought the person wore blue clothing, perhaps the hospital scrubs of a nurse. He kept watching until the room went dark a few minutes later.

Sensing that he'd been right the first time, he refocused on that room, now the only light shining on the floor. Within minutes he saw a shadowy figure pass between the curtains and then disappear; then he saw him go by again, pacing the other way. *That has to be it.*

A few extra minutes of surveillance removed most of his doubt. The figure stepped between the curtains and drew them back slightly. No blue scrubs of a nurse or the white coat of a doctor, the man wore a dark suit. *Bingo.*

Max pulled the Suburban to a space near a side exit that probably accessed a stairwell. Shouldering a small daypack loaded with his supplies, he walked to the door and tried it. Locked, no surprise. He figured it would open from the inside and didn't worry about it further.

He walked around the building, encountering three people smoking near the main entrance. Halting near the glass double doors, he pretended to check his phone while surreptitiously glancing through the high plate-glass windows into the lobby, on the lookout for any agents or security who might be posted. He saw no cops or suits, only a lone security guard in a white uniform stationed by the information desk, monitoring the entrance. Not unusual, the hospital likely posted security there 24-7.

Had the feds given them Max's description? Hard to say, yet certainly probable. A metal-detecting wand hung from the guard's belt. Had the store carried what he'd needed, he would have gone in unarmed; as it stood, he would have to bypass the guard to sneak in the .380 strapped to his ankle.

The three smokers finished their butts and walked toward the door. *Get with the herd.* He held the door open for them, then followed them inside. All three were black, so he didn't exactly fit in, yet he had to try. The lone man in the group mentioned something to one of the women, his wife perhaps, about the Washington Nationals getting a new pitcher via a trade.

"Good thing that happened," Max said. "I was worried the trade wouldn't go through."

"I know, right?" the man responded. He seemed good-natured and talkative enough. "I'm thinkin' he's Cy Young material here in a couple years."

"Me too. And we really need some depth in the bullpen."

The guy fell back next to Max, who got the feeling his wife wasn't much for talking baseball. "They wanna make him a closer, but he might be better as a starter."

"Eh, I wouldn't worry." Max waved a hand. "With that fastball he's gonna be a threat wherever they put him."

"His slider's no slouch either."

Meanwhile, the guard, no doubt bored stiff, had turned his back, talking to the woman at the info desk. Max and his new pal walked past unmolested, though the guard did glance back at them once before he returned to talking up the receptionist. If the feds had given Max's description to security, then his disguise had worked. He had purchased black hair dye and a canister of spray tan at the store and applied them in the restroom, hoping to pass himself off as Hispanic or Mediterranean descent. A pair of horn-rimmed pharmacy reading glasses of minimal magnification completed his disguise. He thought the spray tan made him look more orange than Italian, but if the guard bought it, then others might too.

Still he wasn't about to become complacent. His tall, muscular build might easily betray him to even the dullest federal agent.

Having hurdled the first obstacle, Max stuck with the man for a couple more minutes before bidding farewell, still clueless as to the pitcher's identity. Consulting a map directory on a kiosk, he noted the various stairwells and exits, finding that he'd parked in the best spot. It also confirmed his memory of a ninety-degree turn in the hallway a short distance from Leet's room.

He needed to move quickly. The feds might be watching him even now on monitors in the security control room.

Max looked over the map one final time before he moved. Leet's room wasn't far from the stairway he would have to carry her down. All he needed was a deserted spot on the ground floor not too far from the ER. He studied the map and selected a handicap-only restroom.

Nonchalant, he made the short walk, just another guy at the hospital visiting an injured friend. The never-ending bustle of the ER could be heard down the deserted hallway. He stepped in the bathroom, locked the door, and got to work.

Of the myriad ways to infiltrate a stronghold, the time-tested diversion was still one of the best. This one would be a doozy, though he would have preferred to place the explosives in a more isolated area. He'd wanted to use firecrackers to harmlessly simulate gunfire, but the Commonwealth of Virginia had banned their purchase. Fortunately, the low traffic of a hospital in the dead of night counterbalanced the threat of incidental casualties. If he saw anyone coming when he departed, he would inform them the cleaning staff was busy mopping inside.

No need for concealment, he placed the small block of C-4 and its detonator in the sink, then set the digital timer for two minutes. As he watched the first few seconds tick away on the timer, he ruminated that he was probably wanted for numerous crimes committed during the course of this mission. *Now they can add domestic terrorism to the list.* But it had to be done. Abandoning Leet to the feds was not an option; his conscience would never forgive him. *Fuck it.*

Thankfully, the hallway remained deserted. He walked to the stairwell at the end of the hall, ducked into an alcove before a door labeled PROSTHETICS, the room beyond dark through the window. He pulled the .380 from his ankle holster and waited, watched the seconds count down on his watch.

3… 2…

The report of the explosion was tremendous, as if a howitzer had been fired in the hallway. He stepped from the alcove in the immediate aftermath, saw the door blown off its hinges and lying on the floor just before smoke obscured his view. Screams drifted to him from the ER, total bedlam ensuing. Max fired six shots, erratically spaced, through the window into the prosthetics lab, then turned and hauled ass for the stairs.

* * *

The painkillers in the IV bag hanging next to Leet's bed kept her locked in a constant, groggy high, which would have been nice had they completely eliminated her pain. But they'd taken her off the morphine in the aftermath of her operation. She supposed it was for the best, hospitals finally acknowledging the opioid epidemic and keeping such prescriptions to a minimum.

Her new drugs left her just coherent enough to understand her predicament. Neither of the agents guarding her had explained her situation, but she'd gotten the gist through bits and pieces of their conversation. A warrant had been issued for her arrest, though the charges remained a mystery. She would be moved under guard to a detention facility when the doctor approved her discharge, likely within the next twenty-four hours. Neither agent had attempted to question her; likewise she hadn't spoken to them at all, pretending to be drug addled even when somewhat coherent.

The agents' conversations revealed other things too. Their names: Green and Hobson. She didn't remember meeting either of them, but the name Green rang a bell. It had taken her over an hour to figure it out: he had stolen something from them, which she later remembered was a case full of Monopoly money. After that, other pieces of her previous mission slowly fell into place, though gaping holes still punctured the tale in places. She remembered Shai—how could she ever forget him?—as well as Max something-or-other, her partner after Don died.

Max and Shai were gone now. *Arrested? Probably.* And Shai, she recalled, had turned out to be a robot. *No, that's not the word... android.* She shook her head, held back tears. *Keep him safe, Max, wherever you two are.* She hoped they were free, that Max would do a better job of guarding Shai than she had.

"Christ, this is boring," said Green through his closely cropped black beard. He put down his phone and leaned back in the vinyl chair.

"It'll be over soon," said Hobson, a lanky young agent who stood just inside her door. He would poke his bespectacled face out into the hallway every thirty seconds or so, not quite as vigilant as he'd been during daylight hours, yet a far cry from Green, the complaining veteran. She figured Hobson was new to the Bureau, not much younger than she was, for he still possessed an inexperienced agent's zeal for duty. She also believed he was clean, unassociated with the dirty agents working for Fisher. A tense, distrustful space seemed to separate the two agents, keeping them from gelling and working equally hard as agents on a job should. *I'll use it to my advantage... if I get a chance.*

Then again she might be wrong, Hobson's good character only a drug-induced delusion. But whether she was right or wrong, the young agent plainly believed whatever lies he'd been told about her being a corrupt agent. *Can you blame him? What would you believe if you were in his shoes?*

Green yawned. "Not soon enough. The wheels of justice are slow, rookie. But she's gonna get what's coming to her."

Hobson turned to stare at him. "If she's convicted after due process."

With a chuckle Green said, "Ah yes, forgive me. After due process. Now if you'll excuse me, I'm gonna get some sleep."

"Fire away." Hobson turned his back on Green, stood squarely blocking her door as he scanned the hallway left and right.

A short while later, as Leet began to drift off to sleep, the building shook.

"What the fuck!" Green shouted, popping up from the chair.

"It felt like a bomb!" Hobson said.

Green drew his pistol. "No shit! And I know why. Ahlgren's here."

Leet was inclined to agree with him. Her lips turned up in a faint smile. *Ahlgren, that's his last name.*

"You don't know that for sure!" Hobson shot back. "I'm gonna call it in and request backup. It could be a terror attack."

"Wake the fuck up, rookie; it's him! I know it's him! There's no time for that!"

"I'm gonna go check it out."

"Uh-uh. You're staying right here. That's an order."

Hobson turned away, peeked into the hallway. "You! FBI!" He stepped out and flashed his credential, enough authority to stop the security guard running down the hallway. Chaos crackled through the speaker on the guard's radio. "What's the situation?"

"Bomb exploded, first floor near the ER. Shots fired!"

"We're on it!" the newly minted agent assured him.

“I’m gonna call the office,” Green said, hysterical. “Don’t you fucking leave!”

Hobson gaped at his superior. “We have to investigate. It’s our job. What the fuck is wrong with you?”

Scared shitless, maybe?

Green ignored his question. “You’re gonna stay right—”

“No, I’m going. Your dereliction will be mentioned in my report!”

“Get back…”

Hobson was gone.

“Shit, *shit!*” Green held his phone in one hand, his pistol in the other. He couldn’t decide which to use. His eyes fell on Leet. “What the fuck are you smiling about?” He pointed his pistol at her.

“You’re fucked.”

“And you’re gonna die!” He hit a prompt on his phone and raised it to his ear, keeping the gun on Leet as he stood by the foot of her bed.

A massive figure plowed into the room. It might have been the drugs, but Leet swore she’d never seen a man so large move so fast. Despite his change in appearance, Leet recognized Max quickly enough by his build and his savage fighting style. He slammed into Green, put his shoulder into the agent’s chest, and bowled him back into the wall. Green’s gun arm flailed. He fired two panicked shots, both striking the ceiling. Max pivoted, snatched Green’s right forearm in both hands. An instant later Green was howling, his arm bent thirty degrees. The gun fell from his grasp.

“Oh it’s you!” Though Max growled the words, he sounded quite pleased.

Green landed a punch with his working left arm that tagged Max hard on the chin and snapped his head to the side for an instant. Max didn’t seem to feel it, wasn’t dazed in the slightest. He easily avoided a knee intended for his crotch, then hit Green with the hardest backhand Leet had ever seen, following with punches to the jaw and gut. Blood spattered the antiseptic white walls in nonsensical patterns as the merciless beating continued.

Though no slouch with his fists, Green lacked the height and strength to challenge Max as an equal. Soon he stood pinned to the wall, gasping and bleeding profusely, completely at Max's mercy. Not the place to be. Max seized his broken right arm and hefted Green aloft, took two steps toward the window, and tossed him.

Some last-instant floundering by Green threw off Max's aim so instead of flying through the window to plummet to his death, the squirming man landed with a grunt atop the air conditioning unit. He tried to flop off to escape, only to find himself grabbed and held aloft once again. Max body slammed him to the floor and then proceeded to stomp him into the tiles, kicking his ribs to splinters before finally dropping down to his level.

Leet sat up in bed, a painful ordeal, to get a better view. Max would murder Green, and justly so. She would have loved to see it, but a warning sounded in her head. *No! He can't do that!*

"I've been dreaming of this," Max said before dropping a monstrous right fist into Green's face. He continued to pummel the dirty agent, transforming his mug into bearded and bruised pudding.

When Max poised his thumbs over Green's eyes and prepared to drive them straight into his brain, Leet found the strength to speak. "Max!" The effort of shouting caused her great pain. "Stop! They'll know… know it was you. They'll charge you with murder. Don't!"

Max looked up at her yet didn't say a word. After a few moments he nodded and turned his attention back to Green, thumbs still poised for the killing jabs. "Looks like it's your lucky day." He spat in Green's bloodied and demolished face. "But I wouldn't get used to it. You're on my list, Green. If I were you, I'd skip the country."

With that, Max raised Green's head and then brutally slammed his skull to the floor, knocking him completely senseless. Leet feared that Green would die from the beating alone. And there were other matters to worry over as well.

"Hurry," she said to Max. "The other agent might come back."

"Is he one of them?"

"No, I think he's clean, a rookie."

Like a true professional, Max snapped out of his murderous rage in a heartbeat. "Understood. Let's get you out of here." He rose and moved to her bedside.

A faint, tinny squawk emanated from the floor. Not Green, but rather the phone he'd dropped. "Green?" said the speaker. "Green what the fuck? Status report!"

Max gritted his teeth, face contorted in anger. One mighty stomp of his boot scattered broken bits of smartphone across the floor. "I hope it was insured."

Leet laughed, wincing at the intense pain.

"See that? I'm the best medicine there is." He disconnected her from various monitors and tubes. "Let's get you out of here before the cops show up and cordon this place off."

"I'm with you on that."

Max chuckled. "As if you have a choice."

The pain hit her hard as he lifted her. Out in the hallway people shouted, screamed, cursed, ran about in fear and confusion like a herd of frightened deer. She passed out from the pain before they even reached the stairs.

20

Max sat at the farmhouse table in Otto's rather rustic kitchen, eating bacon and eggs and dreading the upcoming conversation with Leet that was bound to morph into a confrontation.

She had remained unconscious during the drive to North Carolina and for another day after that. Completely drained from battles, chases, and guilt, Max had likewise crashed for nearly twenty-four hours after reaching Otto's house. His trials would resume momentarily, however, for Leet had awakened. He heard muffled voices from down the hall, where she talked behind a closed door with Otto's girlfriend Linda as the nurse saw to her recovery.

"How is she?" Max asked Linda when she entered the kitchen a few minutes later.

"All piss and vinegar," she said from the sink, washing her hands. "She should be up and walking again by tomorrow." Otto had bagged himself one solid woman. *He deserves as much.*

"I can't thank you enough for this."

"You won't say that when I mail you the bill." She smiled at him beneath glistening blue eyes, but the amused expression fell from her face an instant later. "She's asking about the boy. I played it off as best I could, but she knows something's up."

"Sorry to put you on the spot like that. I'm going to tell her right now."

"It's okay; I was expecting it. The first question guys would ask when they woke up in the field hospital was what happened to their buddies." Linda had been a nurse in the Navy for several years before moving back to the civilian world to make a better living. She'd seen her share of ugly shit, trauma both physical and mental, and knew how to approach these matters tactfully. "Try to take it easy on her. She's still in a delicate condition."

"I'll do my best." *It won't be good enough.*

"I'm gonna get ready for work. Where's Otto?"

"Said he was going to the feed store."

She laughed. "He's got plenty of feed. I think he just goes there to bullshit with the old timers."

Otto didn't live off grid per se, but he tried to stay as self-sufficient as possible, which included raising livestock and gardening for most of his food. Max could attest to the quality of his organically produced bacon and eggs. During his time in the corps, Otto had frequently expressed his relief at having escaped the farm life of his youth, a backward existence to hear him tell it at the time. Now the exigencies of a changing world had forced him to revisit his roots on a smaller scale. Max knew from experience how people who escaped the perceived prisons of their youth often returned to them years later.

"You guys have a good thing going. I hate like hell to keep interrupting your lives."

"It's not a problem, Max. Nothing wrong with a little excitement around here now and then."

"There's about to be plenty of that."

"Yep, so I'm gonna disappear now. Good luck."

Max took his time eating the final strip of bacon, then went to drop the bad news on Leet.

She sat upright in bed, a half-finished tray of breakfast on her lap. Her color had improved along with her alertness; perhaps Linda had further reduced her pain medications.

Leet fixed her stare on Max. "Where's Shai? What happened to him?"

"A you're welcome and a pleasant good morning to you too. How do you feel?"

"Like I'm about to be bullshitted by a man unequal to the task. Now where is he?"

Just get it over with. "Gone."

She glared at him. "Where? Who did you leave him with?"

"Just let me talk, okay? It's very involved."

"Fine. I'm waiting."

Max laid it on her: Shai's dark vision of his future, his fears of being used by a corrupt ruling order, of becoming corrupted himself.

Leet remained silent as he spoke. Her glowering gaze said everything.

"We had a heavy conversation." Max paused, looked away as he took a deep breath. "And Shai decided that he needed to be eliminated."

"Eliminated? What the fuck does that mean, Ahlgren? Enough already with the goddamn newspeak." She winced slightly from pain as she spat the questions.

"It means he's gone, Margaret. For good and forever. I'm sorry."

"I don't give a shit if you're sorry. Gone? Where? He needs to be taken—"

"He's dead. I couldn't convince him to keep going, not with the stakes he faced to remain alive."

She shook her head, stared around the room in shock. "You let him commit suicide?" she finally breathed.

"No. He couldn't do it; it was against his programming. I had to—"

"You fucking murdered him."

"I had no choice!" Max raised his voice to just below a shout.

"No choice? Which one of you was a machine, Max? Is your trigger finger on autopilot?"

"Just shut up and listen. It was his request, and I had to honor it. Humanity isn't ready for intelligence like his. He knew it, and he decided it was for the best. And I'm sorry, but you're gonna have to deal with it. Do you think I enjoyed—"

"Get out! Get the fuck outta my sight, or so help me I'll send you to join him." Her purse and the sidearm within sat on the nightstand in easy reach.

"Fine." Max went to leave yet turned halfway around as he headed out the door.

"You forget something, asshole?"

"You know, you've scolded me a couple of times about losing my bearing. Well, you need to find yours and accept Shai's final wish. It's over, Margaret, and it was for the best. I wish you could see that, but I don't need you to."

"Get out!"

Without a further glance backward, Max did just that.

* * *

Max hadn't been on a working farm in decades, not since his grandfather's passing. This didn't stop him from spending the afternoon helping Otto slop hogs, feed chickens, and pick apples. He was still pretty banged up from the mission, but he knew that lying in bed would only delay his recovery. The chores were the definition of drudgery, just the sort of grueling work he needed to take his mind off Leet and Shai, though he couldn't call his efforts totally successful in that department.

"She'll come around," Otto said as they sat on his deck having a beer at the end of the workday. "You did the right thing. I've done a lot of research into AI, and that boy was light years ahead of everything else produced to this point. Hell, I still can't believe I didn't recognize an actual android when he was staying in my house."

"He was way past that. Maybe not human, but I can't think of him as an android. He had emotions, maybe even a soul, whatever that is."

Otto shook his head. "It never fails, Max. They take everything they can and destroy what they can never possess."

No need to ask who *they* were. "They only destroyed him in the metaphorical sense. I was the trigger man, like so many times before."

"Somebody had to do it. Stop misreading your moral compass. True leaders accept and move on. I know it's easy for me to say, but you know the truth. Hell, I learned it from you."

"I can't argue with that."

Otto gave a curt nod. "Stick by the decision. She'll come to accept it."

"I sure as hell hope so."

"Count on it. She's a good one; she'll figure it out."

Though the conversation turned to lighter things, Max only hung out for one beer, guilt still lingering in his mind. He went inside for a shower to wash off the stink of the barnyard.

His phone vibrated while he was drying off. *Marklin.* Out of dire necessity, Max had phoned his most powerful ally on the way to North Carolina, though their dilemma might be something even he couldn't resolve. "Good evening, General."

"You sound a little depressed, son," Marklin said. "Buck up. One of us shot eleven over par today, you know."

Max hadn't known. And he didn't give a shit about Marklin's golf game. "My condolences. I hope that was after you spoke to the senator."

"You know I'm business first, Ahlgren. And I have good news. The charges and warrants on you and Special Agent Leet have been dropped. Good thing the senator likes you; she had to kiss ass and whip ass to get it done. She also alerted the FBI and CIA directors regarding the activities of these operatives who were after your project. What will come of that is anyone's guess, but you two are off scot free as long as you keep this matter private."

"That won't be an issue. I can't thank you enough, General."

"Save it. Thank the senator next time you see her, and remember you owe her one… hell, maybe half a dozen."

"I figured we'd be about even. But I guess we both know that's never the case." The senator had been indebted to him for saving her son from Gideon Wilde, but gratitude only went so far, especially in the halls of government. Max hated owing anyone anything; however, the senator had pulled off a miraculous feat. If she ever needed his services again, he would be there with wings on his heels and a smile on his face.

"Now go on back to Vegas and stay the hell out of trouble. I don't want to hear from you again for a long time… unless you want to try me on the skeet range."

"Maybe so. Somebody has to humble you, eventually."

"When I want to be humbled, I play golf. Now, if you'll excuse me, I need to get back to my regularly scheduled life." He terminated the call.

Maybe that'll cheer her up. Something had to, eventually. But Max was in no mood to tell her just yet, knowing full well that she would tongue lash him again if he entered her room.

And he had other business to take care of, a pressing matter that he'd been forced to put off for far too long.

Max got dressed, opened his laptop, and took a seat at the small desk in the guest room. He plugged in a flash drive with the Tails operating system, a necessity for accessing the dark web. Once online, he logged into his TorChat profile. Only two emails awaited him. The first was from a private investigator in Australia, whom Max had retained to check out a lead pertaining to his family's killers. The man had produced no new results and demanded a deposit for further work if Max wished to keep him on. Max messaged back, thanked him for his efforts, despite the lack of useful information, and released him from service.

The second was from a user he didn't recognize: Wunderkind_16037. Max opened the email.

Max:

I hope the attached files will be of use to you. And if you must act, I know it shall be with a prudent and measured sense of justice and not merely a raging thirst for revenge. Be warned that this is bigger than you could have imagined.

Give Margaret my love…

Shai

I won't let you down, Shai. Max considered the files: two jpegs sandwiching a website link. Assuming that Shai meant for them to be revealed in order, he clicked on the first jpeg.

Even via the ultra-fast satellite internet system custom built by Otto, the picture took a few seconds to download. *Must be super high-res,* Max mused as the photo took shape, gradually crawling down and filling the screen. When finished, the photo shrunk to smaller proportions. He clicked on the photo to enlarge it. High-res was an understatement; the picture measured several thousand pixels per side. Max dragged it around the screen and studied each individual portion in detail. It looked like a mug shot, only the brown-haired young man in the gray suit was not a merc or a criminal, at least according to the government. This was an official CIA photo taken at the beginning of this operative's career. They had taken Max's photo as well, as they did with all new operatives. Pertinent information about the agent was listed beneath the photo. Jonathan Horace Godshall, born 3 March 1973 in Boston, Massachusetts. Other information followed: social security number, CIA ID number, fingerprints, physical statistics such as height, weight, hair and eye color. The photo dated from September 1997.

Max studied the photo again, paying particular attention to the man's physiognomy. *I've never seen him before.* He could have sworn it on a stack of bibles; nevertheless, he saved it to a file he kept specifically for his quest.

He moved on to the link, a line of garbled letters and numbers followed by .onion, which linked to a page on a dark web site titled *Stooges of the Statists.* "Isn't this interesting..." The page's stated purpose was to out known operatives of covert intelligence organizations worldwide in the ongoing interests of, "Killing one-world government *before* it starts, one agent at a time."

Sadly, despite having known a few upstanding men in the Agency, it sounded to Max like a noble effort. Indeed, one in which he'd unwittingly participated—he had personally tortured and then murdered the second man on the list, Chris Darling, aka Charles Dawes, right-hand man to Peter Banner. *I should let them know so they can update the page.* He smiled, remembering the satisfaction and sadistic glee he'd taken in making Darling's final moments on earth a waking nightmare. He bookmarked the page; the information might come in handy sometime.

More names and photos of agents followed, running the gamut of world intelligence organizations: CIA, MI6, Mossad, BND, and a couple of others. Two of them looked vaguely familiar, yet none were Jonathan Godshall.

Max found him at the bottom of the page, the literal last man.

He studied the grainy black-and-white shot of a man who had raised his jacket slightly too late to avoid his face being photographed. It looked as though he was walking down the steps of a courthouse or some other marble-covered government building. "Whoa..."

Max often thought of General Marklin as the man who had inducted him into the CIA, yet that wasn't entirely accurate. Marklin had been the Marine Corps liaison to the CIA and had given Max the option to join in lieu of a death sentence. The company man who had actually inducted him—and given Max his first lesson in effectively and efficiently torturing a man—looked out wide-eyed from beneath a flapping coat.

The caption beneath the photo read: "Photo taken 7/23/2004 Washington DC by a *Washington Post* photographer, as Jonathan Goadish—his name at the time—departed a hearing of the Senate Intelligence Committee. The photo was never published and was ordered destroyed. True name unknown. Aliases: Jacob Goodman, Jerome Gamble, Jonathan Goadish, John Goebel."

Along with inventing several aliases, Jonathan Godshall had received plastic surgery at some point between 1997 and 2004 and barely resembled his induction photo. Differences included his hairline, a slight widow's peak of black hair in the second photo replacing the straight line of brown at induction, along with cheek implants and a nose job. Beneath the caption, the writer listed various crimes attributed to Godshall, who had been Mr. Goadish when Max met him in 2006. Most allegations involved attempts to overthrow Third World regimes around the globe, some of them successful. This man had operated around the globe, and where he went Hell followed. The governments of Yemen and Eritrea had warrants out for his capture, dead or alive.

At least I know where not *to look for him. But where the hell is he now?*

The last piece of information provided by Shai, a Brazilian driver's license issued only three months ago, provided Max with some particulars, though he did not expect to find a man as elusive and shady as Goadish at the listed address in the city of Belo Horizonte. He called himself Johannes Gutmann these days. He'd put on a little weight and undergone more plastic surgery. His nose appeared to have been broken once or twice. His once-luxuriant head of hair had been sacrificed in the interest of national security, diminished to a sparse ring of gray surrounding the bald crown Max had seen fleeing the warehouse.

Goadish soldiered on beneath the façade.

That Goadish was involved with the plot didn't surprise Max, and he wondered how he'd never considered him before. He could only chalk it up to unfamiliarity. Max had only met him one time. *Yeah, but the son of a bitch was unforgettable.*

"Christ, you are a hard-fucking sell, you know that?" Goadish had told Max on that long-ago day, after which he'd whipped off the hood covering the face of the man in the chair, Max's first torture victim.

And fuck did I enjoy it.

Whitbeck had been his name, Max's superior officer on his last mission as a Marine, the man who had accidentally killed their commanding officer. He blamed it on Max, calling it murder.

Max could only remember feeling thankful to Goadish after he'd revealed Whitbeck. Perhaps that was why he had never considered him. *That's not a good enough reason.* After serving for a couple of months in the Agency, he'd learned not to trust anyone, no matter what favors they did for him.

But Max was done beating himself up over perceived negligence. Shai's information had narrowed his search, albeit to an area of several million square miles. *But I'll find him.* Scheming pieces of shit like Goadish weren't that hard to locate, if one knew where to begin. *Start searching in the hallowed halls of the Brazilian government, then follow the breadcrumbs.*

EPILOGUE

They trudged through pine scrub and sandy soil as the eastern sky reddened before the dawn.

"This is quite a trek," said Leet, who walked behind Max. She sounded a bit winded, still not fully recovered from the gunshot wound she'd taken a week before but getting there fast. "You're pretty good at hiding bodies in the woods."

"I learned many skills in the Agency, some more practical than others."

They hiked on in silence, each lost in memory, or so Max assumed. They had been hunted for slightly over four days by the forces of multiple governments, yet Max still felt as though he'd survived a protracted military campaign. Not so much in a physical sense—he'd taken more grievous injuries on many a mission—but on a deeper mental level. Pulling the trigger on Shai still haunted him and probably always would. Leet's condemnation of his actions had weighed on him as well, even though she apologized the next day. Though barely able to walk, she flew to Michigan shortly after that, arriving just in time to attend Don Wagner's funeral.

Meanwhile, Max had returned to DC to make arrangements for Daniel Farber. He couldn't take a gunshot victim to a funeral home and expect them not to ask questions, so again Marklin helped him out, arranging for a discreet cremation at a government morgue under the guise of natural causes. To discourage operatives from continuing the chase, news of Daniel's death, again due to natural causes, had been released to the press.

Leet carried the brass urn containing Daniel's ashes, while Max shouldered the shovel. *This is the last time I bury an innocent man.* He liked to think so, anyway. *No, there will be others, unfortunately. I won't get to Goadish and Jarvis without help.* Max could only hope to keep friendly casualties to a minimum.

Soon they reached the stand of pines atop the low rise overlooking the cove. Leet looked around, saw the freshly turned earth marking Shai's grave, gazed up into the pines and out over the water. "It's beautiful. You chose a nice spot."

"Yeah. This is a special place for me."

"For both of us."

Max nodded. "Yes, it is."

He dug a hole roughly two feet deep as Leet looked on. When the time came to place the urn, Max said, "I don't do prayers, Margaret. I've seen too much senseless slaughter in my life to believe they work. But if you have anything to say—"

"I will… but not a prayer. Something afterward. I haven't had a chance to say goodbye."

"I understand."

They placed the urn in the earth. Max buried it, then stepped from the pines to watch the sunrise, leaving Leet alone at the grave. He wondered, as the sun breached the horizon in brilliant and blinding beams, if Janet's soul ever wandered to this primeval place that he held so much in reverence. *If so, she'll be in good company.*

As for Jonathan Goadish and Burt Jarvis, he vowed that neither would come to know any semblance of eternal peace, wherever he happened to bury them. If there was a Hell, he would follow them there to make sure they burned.

Leet came to him a short time later. Neither said a word at first as they sat watching the sunrise. "I'm sorry." She wiped an errant tear from her cheek. "I know I said it before, but this time I really mean it."

"You know that's not necessary. I'm just satisfied that you understand now."

"I shouldn't have questioned your—no, *his* decision."

"I questioned it too," Max admitted. "How could I not? Hey, you feeling all right?"

"Yeah. It all feels… I don't know, *appropriate* for some reason, even though it's not right. Any of it."

"I get it. And it won't be the last time for either of us unfortunately. Unless you're planning to leave the Bureau."

Leet scoffed at the idea. "No way. I'm there for life, however long I have left."

"Good. You're the kind of agent this country needs. And if you're ever in deep trouble, you know where to find me."

"Thanks."

"You're welcome. I don't work with just anyone, but I'd work with you again anytime."

Max helped her to her feet, and they began the long trek back to the car. They passed the grave again, neither stopping. Due respects had been paid; time for all concerned to move on.

Taking a last glance at the final resting place of Shai and Daniel, Max noticed something bright lying atop the sand and pine needles.

A lone white rose.

ABOUT THE AUTHOR

Ryan Aslesen is a bestselling author and security consultant based out of Las Vegas, NV. He is a former Marine officer, veteran of the War on Terror, and a graduate of Presentation College and American Military University. His military and work experience have made him one of the premier writers of military science fiction. His bestselling Crucible Series is highly regarded for its authenticity, explosive action, and sci-fi twists. When not writing or out protecting the world, you will find him spending quality time with his family. He is currently working on his next novel. He can be reached at ryan.w.aslesen@gmail.com

Check out Max's other adventures in the bestselling Crucible Series.

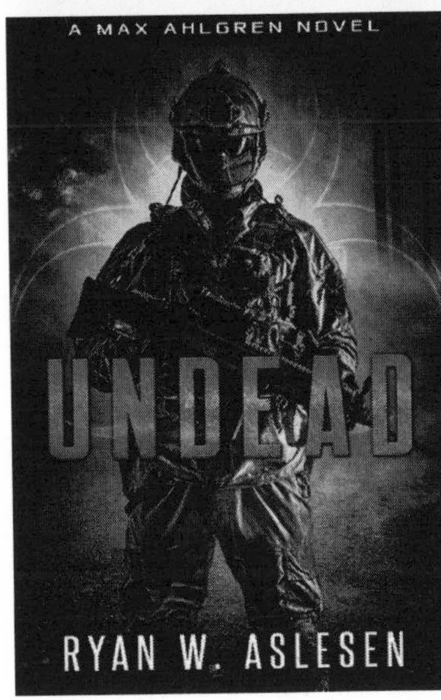